In Search of Your Soul

The Beginning of the Journey

Helga Polman

Prologue

It was starting to rain outside, and the wind was picking up. Wrapped in my coat, I walked down to the road and suddenly heard a growl a meter away. I remembered the enclosures I had seen when I came here and their size. Freezing and without any sudden movements, I raised my head at the source of the sound and immediately regretted my decision to leave the house. In front of me stood a huge Doberman with a grin, and behind him, two more were slowly approaching. My whole life flashed before my eyes, and for a second, I was sad to realize how little I managed to do in it.

"Stop! Get back to your place!"

Alex's voice was so sharp and loud that I jumped on the spot.

The dogs flattened their ears and obediently followed the command.

"Thank you," I said, barely audibly.

"Let's go inside. A little more, and you'll get wet," surprisingly softly and with care, my savior said.

I turned around, and a new wave of shock hit me. Alex was standing there with only a towel tied around his hips, which was trying to slip off his oblique abdominal muscles. Raindrops fell on his firm chest, pumped torso, and strong arms. His black, wet hair fell over his incredibly handsome face. His bushy black eyebrows, blue eyes, chiseled cheekbones, and plump scarlet lips were maddening. Everything about this man was perfect.

No, I'd rather go back to the dogs. I'll definitely forget about principles and morals with this man. I told myself.

CONTENTS

CHAPTER 1 7
CHAPTER 2 13
CHAPTER 3 18
CHAPTER 4 23
CHAPTER 5 28
CHAPTER 6 33
CHAPTER 7 39
CHAPTER 8 45
CHAPTER 9 50
CHAPTER 10 57
CHAPTER 11 63
CHAPTER 12 69
CHAPTER 13 74
CHAPTER 14 79
CHAPTER 15 84
CHAPTER 16 88
CHAPTER 17 93
CHAPTER 18 99
CHAPTER 19 104
CHAPTER 20 109
CHAPTER 21 115
CHAPTER 22 121
CHAPTER 23 128
CHAPTER 24 135
CHAPTER 25 141
CHAPTER 26 144
CHAPTER 27 150
CHAPTER 28 154
CHAPTER 29 158
CHAPTER 30 163
CHAPTER 31 166
CHAPTER 32 171
CHAPTER 33 174
CHAPTER 34 181

Chapter 1

The room was filled with the warm light from the fireplace, creating a warm and cozy atmosphere, the logs crackling peacefully and driving the depressing thoughts from my mind. Slowly, I swirled the whiskey glass in my hand, watching the drops flow down in a thin, wriggling line.

The muffled clatter of heels could be heard in the hallway. One could tell by the frequency of the sound that the owner of that gait was walking confidently. The door creaked softly and opened.

"How did they let you in here? The manager said it was a private club, and no one could disturb me," I asked with a smirk, knowing there were no closed doors for this woman.

"And I'm glad to see you," she kissed me on the cheek and sat on the chair at my side.

"What can I pour you?" I asked politely.

"Something light. We'll move on to the heavy stuff after the case."

In her beautiful blue eyes, the devils were running.

"Hmm... And what business brought you here?" I handed Lika a shot of her favorite drink, mint liqueur.

"You know exactly why I'm here. It's time. A year has passed."

"Really? How quickly the year has flown by..."

I went to the fireplace, took a poker, and started stirring the logs.

When I stirred the charred wood, I made sparks fly upward, which soared and flickered in the air. I enjoyed watching this dance of fire, which had always fascinated me.

"I feel weird that I'm the one who's been looking for

you. Mostly, you show up at the appointed time and enter the fray with excitement in your eyes."

"Lika, I'm not an adventurous boy anymore. You know how this year has worn me out. I'm not sure if I want to continue this childishness."

Turning to my sister, I looked into her eyes cautiously. I didn't want to upset her since we'd been playing this game since we were kids. It seemed to be the thread that still bound us together. Over the years, we'd grown apart, but, as time went on, the game got a little too intense. And when life's about to knock you down, you don't need that extra dose of adrenaline.

"Alex, I know you've worked hard this year to keep your company. Although, I will remind you that I offered you an installment plan. But you're so proud that you chose to give up 20% of your company just to do it alone. You even refused Dan's help."

My opponent shook her head.

"I intend to continue. This game is the kind of magic kick that sometimes you just need."

"I thought the last round was really hard on you. I was sure you didn't even want to continue," I snickered.

Last time, we bet on whether my sister could survive six months on a waitress's salary, working honestly for the entire period. The stakes were high, and to my surprise, she not only lived those six months by all the rules but managed to become the receptionist of that establishment quite quickly. As a result, in the last two months, she could pay for a separate apartment, tiny but separate from her neighbors, which was the most important and difficult challenge for her. And since there was no violation of any established rules, I had to pay every penny of the agreed amount. As a consequence, this year became a struggle for my own company. My overconfidence has played tricks on me.

"You're right. It's been extremely difficult for me. There were moments when I wanted to drop everything, get in my favorite car, and drive to the mansion. But you know what stopped me?"

She turned her head to the side and looked at me with big blue eyes. Her blonde hair fell over her shoulder.

"I guess the prize money kept you firmly in place," I said ironically, taking a scalding sip of my drink.

"That's exactly what I expected you to say. What else could a man who spends his entire conscious life solely on increasing his wealth say?" Lika sighed.

I wanted to answer her, but she did not let me continue her admonition.

"But that's the wrong answer and the right one you'll find out for yourself. At least, that's what I'm hoping..."

"Lika, we're not children anymore. I know you've been patronizing me for too long, and it's simply become a habit. You want to change my lifestyle, but at least try to accept the idea that I'm okay with it."

"This conversation, alas, will lead nowhere. It is possible to convey something to you only by action."

Lika sighed heavily.

"I want to show you how much you're missing out. Yes, this world depends on money, but just filling your pockets doesn't make you richer emotionally. Look, no amount of money can cover the hole in your soul."

"Look, I don't have the energy or the time for another bet. Whatever you're trying to tell me, I don't need it right now."

"What if I told you that Villa Del Rado would be at stake this time?"

"Are you kidding?"

I looked into her eyes. She knew how much I desired to get that piece of land.

Why now, exactly, is she willing to risk it? Angelica must be up to an elaborate game, but whatever it is, it's definitely worth it, I thought.

"There's that gambling look. I take it you are in?" Angelica asked cheerfully.

"Would you be so kind as to state the terms," settling back in my chair, I directed my full attention to my interlocutor.

Two days have passed since I met with Lika. There was a lot of work today, like always, but my thoughts were occupied with the villa. I couldn't think about anything else. I was confused — such a prize and yet such an elementary task. Any minute now, Lika was to appear with a notary, who had to check and notarize all the documents.

Rising from my chair, I felt my back and neck stiffen.

Too bad my workout at the gym is postponed today. But, very soon, I'll get to a winery in southern Italy, and it will be completely at my disposal. That thought made a smile spread across my face.

"I see you're all excited."

Immersed in my thoughts, I didn't notice how Lika had entered the office.

"It's so good to see you. You look just dazzling today."

"Ah, how nice to hear. It's a pity it's all pretense," Lika twisted her mouth, and we laughed.

I've forgotten the last time I was in such a marvelous mood.

"Let's get down to business, shall we?"

I rubbed my hands together and took a seat at the head of the table. The guests sat on either side of me.

"Mr. Heifetz, have you read the contract?"

"Yes, Mr. Frai. All the clauses are clear. All I need are your signatures and my seal. Have you discussed all the points of the deal?"

The notary gave me a meaningful look.

This question made me tense. I have known Gidon Heifetz for a long time. For many years, all significant papers have gone through him exclusively. He's a man of his word and incredibly pedantic, which is a great advantage in his work. And if a question like that comes from him, you have to get to the bottom. And I'd be surprised if it was as simple as my sister told me earlier.

"Hand me the contract," I asked, frowning.

Taking the papers, I glanced at my sister. But she was completely calm. It wasn't surprising — she knew I would do anything to get the villa.

I scrutinized every page. In the paragraphs, everything was as discussed before, but the appendix was twice the size of the contract itself and contained many new terms.

"It would take me at least half an hour to study the papers in more detail."

The great mood began to fade rather quickly. It smelled like a trick.

"Al, are you saying anything is stopping you on your way to your goal?" Lika asked with a smug grin.

"It's unlikely, but I don't habitually leave my signature on unchecked papers."

"Mr. Frai, I've spent much time studying every letter in these documents. If you'd like, I'll give you the highlights."

I trusted Gidon as much as I trusted myself, and his suggestion could save us time.

"I would be very grateful to you."

I put the papers aside and looked at the notary.

"The basic agreement is that you need to induce three different girls to have intimate relations for money. For each girl, you have a maximum of three weeks. Their fee is unlimited, but payment will come from your personal funds. Two girls are chosen at random by Mrs. Masters. One girl will be chosen at random by you..."

"Gidon, please familiarize me with the attachment. I have no questions about the main part."

I was beginning to lose patience as I wondered what my one and only sister, Mrs. Masters, could have come up with.

"The appendix is just that if one of the girls refuses, no matter which one it is, you will need to live in the same place with her for six months," Heifetz said with one eyebrow raised.

What is her grand plan? No, of course. I'm used to privacy. But I can tolerate a roommate for such a prize.

This question continued to plague me.

"Lika, let's go straight to the pitfalls. And let's not waste time testing my patience for strength."

"Alex, your patience has grown with you. When you were a boy, you barely had any. But as a man, it seems to me you've learned to wait. You don't know how much I love seeing that boy's curiosity in you again."

A smile spread across her face, but my good mood vanished completely. Apparently, my sister realized from the look on my face that I was about to explode, so she hurried to continue.

"Okay, look, it's all spelled out right here."

Lika found the right page and handed it to me. The documents stated that I had to live in the same house with my neighbor and spend with her all off-duty time, training, and meals. In addition, we must sleep in the same bed. At this point, I coughed and raised my horrified eyes to my sister.

"You're going overboard. Six months without sleep could render me insane. Perhaps we can dispense with that clause?" I asked with hope in my voice.

It would be silly to expect it to be as simple as my sister had presented it to me the last time we met. But I always slept alone. The presence of someone in my bed implied a lack of proper sleep.

"Al, I'm not changing that. It's up to you. Nobody said it was going to be easy. And you'll have my man in your house to report to me on compliance."

Her eyes literally glowed with smugness.

"And besides, aren't you the one who said that everything in this world can be bought and sold? You just have to name the right price. If you really believe that, then you have nothing to fear."

I was unable to respond to this attack.

"There are a couple more points you should pay

attention to," Heifetz broke the silence and turned to me.

I took a deep breath, rubbed my temple tiredly, stood up, and walked towards the bar. Pouring a glass of whiskey, I took a big gulp.

I need to weigh everything up. I'm sure it wouldn't be hard to talk three people into sex for money. But knowing my sister, there's no way around it, so we need to be prepared for any outcome, I said to myself.

Chapter 2

(on behalf of Anna)

It was a wonderful day. The air smelled of spring. Nature was waking from its winter sleep, spreading green buds and replacing grayness with a riot of colors. The sun was shining brightly, warming me with long-awaited warmth. The birds sang, diluting the city noise with a pleasant chirp. This weather was perfect for a walk in the fresh air.

Munich is an incredible city that is so easy to fall in love with, as it turns out. I can't even believe now that I was so resistant to coming three years ago. The local architecture is simply marvellous. It's impossible to walk down the street without closer looking at each house. Of course, the box houses that are familiar to my eye are also present here, but even they look neat. I especially like the absence of skyscrapers. There are a few tall buildings, but their presence does not spoil the overall view and does not create a sense of pressure. And the biggest plus, undoubtedly, is the many parks, in which it is so easy to hide from the endless city bustle and noise, enjoying peace.

Today, fortunately for me, there were few clients, and already at lunchtime, I managed to free myself. My best friend, Julia Anderson, had also snuck out of work due to feeling unwell. She and I are sisters in misfortune. We have Saturday as a work day. In the last couple of weeks, we've both been so busy that we haven't been able to get out for a walk. Even at work, we could barely exchange a few words. It felt like there was no life outside of work.

I had an early morning shift at the beauty salon where I worked as a makeup artist. After that, I rushed to the restaurant where I worked as a waitress and came home late at night. A short nap and in the morning all over again. The fatigue had built up so much lately that it was felt not only on a physical level but also on an emotional level. And not to go crazy, a walk with her friend was the best cure for overstrain.

"Anna, you're in your own thoughts again, and I'm trying to complain about life," Julie jokingly poked me in the shoulder with her finger.

"I'm sorry. Spring is so warm and sunny this time. It seems impossible to be unhappy on days like this," I smiled broadly at my friend.

We stood on the bridge, where the warm breeze was trying hard to tangle my long hair. I'd decided a thousand times to cut it off, but when it came down to it, I couldn't dare.

"That's easy for you to say. You've got everything — a job you love, a husband. What do I have? I'm 25, still single, and I want the comforts of home so badly."

Julie sighed heavily. And I remembered my marriage, and my good mood quickly began to fray.

I shook my head absentmindedly, as if trying to shake off a pesky fly. Of course, I had my favorite job, but that didn't mean I always enjoyed it. If you don't have a proper vacation, sometimes you completely forget how much you used to enjoy it.

"Is that all happiness is?" I asked and reached for her camera, "look at how great it turned out. You have a great talent. You have found something to do for your soul, and soon, you can make a living at it."

"You see, talent is great, but it's lonely and cold in bed alone," she smiled crookedly and continued, "I want to come home and see that I'm welcome. I want to sit down on the couch with my loved one, watch my favorite TV series, and then discuss it all evening, sharing impressions of the day. And at night, if I have a nightmare, I want to cuddle and calm down in the arms of my beloved."

"So, that's enough," I grabbed my companion's hand and pulled her towards the center.

But her words partly affected me. Maybe I wanted the same thing. Things hadn't been as rosy in my marriage for a long time as Julie had imagined.

Although, maybe I'm asking for too much? flashed through my head.

"I know what would cheer you up," I looked at my friend conspiratorially, and her eyes sparkled.

"A vanilla bun!" Julia read my thoughts and perked up.

"And the most delicious latte," I added.

It was a kit in case of sadness. The bun was delicious but incredibly caloric. So we only resorted to it in case of an emergency.

As we walked briskly down the block and turned the corner, we immediately smelled the aroma of our favorite coffee shop that filled the small alleyway. Our hiding place was not so easy to find. But a long time ago, we were somehow lucky enough to find this little oasis in the middle of the very center of the city — a stone road, curly ivy on the walls, and very nice paintings on the street walls.

After ordering, we settled at a table outside and asked for plaids. It wasn't warm enough from the sun yet to feel comfortable.

"Julie, you always complain about how bad it is at home without a man. But you've had a different guy every month for the past year, and you haven't been able to get along with anyone for more than a week. Don't you think you're contradicting yourself a little bit?"

I wanted to choose the right words not to offend my

friend.

"Anna, don't be ridiculous. You're right. It's hard without a man at home, but the key word is a "man." I can't say that these young men are men, because this word has to be earned. At the first meeting, of course, they try to make a good impression, but after just a couple of weeks of joint life and everything — the truth immediately comes to the surface. The last one, Ben, by the way, for the longest time pretended to be a male, the earner, but such a pig turned out to be. After five days of living together, he stopped cleaning up after himself. He couldn't even carry a cup to the dishwasher. And on my proposal to hire a domestic helper, since we both work, he happily agreed until I mentioned that we would pay in half since we live together. A week later, he disappeared. Tell me, is that a man? And this is just one of many this year. And it's not like I'm asking for much. I just want a fair division of responsibilities equally," said my friend, with a heavy sigh, and her gaze was sad again.

The buns arrived just in time — Julie was already recounting all her recent romances. I really wanted to make her happy, but it was beyond me to listen to her go on and on about what I'd heard so many times before. That muffin occupied her mouth for a while, thus giving me a break.

Right after the snack, I reminded her of the high-calorie content of the food, and we decided to move on to walking around the center looking for beautiful angles and, at the same time, spreading out a bit of what we had eaten. Julia didn't really have to fight for her figure, though. She was one of the lucky ones who could eat without affecting her size. But I, alas, was not so fortunate. I'm not complaining about my figure. In my twenty-three years and at a height of one hundred and seventy centimeters, I had graceful forms, a thin waist, firm breasts, and a good butt. But in my case, the main rule was that a solid meal meant a long walk. Otherwise, a lightning-fast plus to centimeters in undesirable places was guaranteed.

We spent three hours running around the squares and streets, but the paparazzi didn't get as many good shots as she would have liked.

"It's not right," Julie summarized. "Listen, everything looks good, but there's nothing to catch the eye. I don't know how to explain it."

"Maybe your eyes, arms, and your legs need a rest," I begged.

"I'm sorry, I got carried away. It's a pity it's useless, although some photos might be appropriate for a portfolio."

Julie showed me the photos. I thought they were great.

"I think someone's being too hard on themselves," I said. "Let's take a break. I heard there's a concert on Stashus tonight, and it starts in half an hour. What do you think?"

"Sounds great," my friend answered.

It took a short drive to our destination, but there was no sign of the concert when we arrived.

"I think I got something wrong," I said guiltily. "And I'm thirsty, so I should get some water. My mouth felt like a branch of the Sahara Desert."

"That's true. Let me quickly run for water, and you sit down. You look tired."

Julie took pity on me, handed me her camera, and sat me down on one of the stone blocks that lined the fountain. After, she went in search of life-giving moisture. I put the camera in my lap, closed my eyes, and put my hands behind my back, leaning on them. Then I threw my head back, exposing my face to the sun.

After a couple of minutes, I got a strange feeling. I felt uncomfortable. I felt like someone was staring at me. Furthermore, I straightened up and looked around but didn't see anything unusual.

Chapter 3

(on behalf of Alex)

Today, it was my turn to choose since Lika had made hers two days ago and pointed to a girl with whom, to my delight, everything went quickly and easily. My sister had chosen a pretty young girl, looking no more than twenty years old. She stood out from the crowd with her well-chosen image, including things from the latest collections of famous fashion houses, had a beautiful posture, and moved in the flow of people quite gracefully.

I think that Lika thought the girl was wealthy enough. It meant the girl would either refuse the offer and I would have to live with someone for the next six months, or she would squeeze a tidy sum out of me. But my sister overlooked a small detail, which, in turn, played into my hands. The girl had a small Fendi bag on her shoulder. I must admit that the copy was of good quality, but only a slight asymmetry on the handle fasteners gave away the fake.

I didn't hesitate. I went to process the victim and invited the lovely creature for a coffee. It was clear that there was no point in beating around the bush. So I went straight to the point. Mila, which was the girl's name, was indeed from a well-to-do family. But in recent months, she had fallen out with her relatives, and they, in turn, deprived her of funding. I wondered about the bag. The young lady explained that she was studying to be a designer at a prestigious university, and her pride did not allow her to wear the same clothes. And since she didn't have enough money for new clothes, she had to find a way out.

I did not go into the details, as they did not interest me much, but I emphasized the main point — the lady did not have enough money to live on. The only thing left to do was to name the right amount, enough to drown out her conscience and principles. Having inquired about monthly habitual expenses, I multiplied it by twelve and voiced this sum to her. My proposal at first shocked her, but after some, she agreed.

I had to follow the terms and not violate the established rules because a mistake could lead to defeat, and therefore, the transfer of my sister thirty-one percent of the company.

I couldn't afford to lose the controlling interest — not so long ago, I had to sell twenty percent of the company when my brainchild was in danger of bankruptcy. Furthermore, I didn't want the stock to go on the market, but this move would bring in new assets, enriching the company many times more.

We agreed to meet Mila in the evening in one of the most expensive hotels in Munich.

At first, I didn't want to get intimate with the girl. I was used to satisfying my sexual hunger with escort girls. They were personally selected by me, knew my preferences, how to give me maximum pleasure, and what exactly should not be done. Most importantly, there was complete safety of contact with them. But the prize was worth all the inconvenience.

I met the girl in the best hotel room at the appointed time to make the right impression. First, I handed over the bank card with all the details, so Mila could check the balance. Once she was sure there was no cheating, she calmed down a bit but was still anxious, which wasn't surprising given the circumstances.

I calmly walked over to her and ran my hand over her cheek. The skin was soft and velvety. Placing my thumb on her chin, I lifted her face. Mila's eyes displayed mixed feelings. I could feel her fear but also desire. I was used to this combination of feelings. Almost all women experienced them when in intimate proximity to me. I placed one hand on her waist, and with the other, stroking with my fingertips, I moved along her neck, accompanying my touches with kisses. The girl bit her lip, and her breathing began to quicken. A predatory smile stretched across my face. It was amusing to watch this fragile girl. Her body responded so vividly to my touch. Barely touching, I ran my hand along the curve of her back, and she was already trembling in my arms. When I bit her earlobe and ran the tip of my tongue along the inside of her ear, she arched and moaned with pleasure. With each new wave of her excitement, I gained more and more power over her.

Mila was no longer able to stand on her feet. Her eyes were clouded with passion. Taking her in my arms, I carried her to the bedroom, where she nestled against my lips. But I interrupted the hot kiss and began to remove her clothes slowly. The girl was wearing a black mini-dress, and it wasn't hard to get rid of it. Which gave me full access to the beautiful young body, parts of which were barely covered by lacy lingerie.

Positioning Mila on the bed, I hung over her, studying every line of her perfect body. I savored the sight of her breasts heaving so rapidly from her frequent breathing and the way her embarrassment vanished without a trace, replaced by lust.

For a moment, I caught myself thinking that I enjoyed torturing her, pushing her to the limit, and wincing as I watched the growing madness in those gray-blue eyes. I enjoyed watching her greedily gulping air with her mouth and digging her hands into the sheet.

With escort girls, everything had long been a pattern, and I was more than satisfied with it, but maybe Lika was right about something - I was beginning to forget the taste of life. The feeling of novelty was exciting.

I pulled down the lacy panties with ease, ran my fingertips along the inside of her thigh and moved upward. Mila almost gasped at my touch. Her breath hitched, and the room filled with the sensual moans of a girl wriggling under me, eager for direct continuation.

When I'd had enough, I shed my clothes and pressed my naked body against her hot, goosebump-covered skin. I covered her lips in a long kiss, savoring how the most sensitive parts of our bodies touched. She arched toward me, accepting me. Overwhelmed, the girl tried to cling to my broad back, but our bodies were heated and wet with sweat. So she slipped away, leaving red streaks of passion on my skin. Mila bit my shoulders, moaning, screaming, and begging me not to stop. I couldn't limit myself to one time. Getting into the excitement, I wanted more and more. Finally, exhausted and satisfied, we froze in silence.

Quietly, trying not to disturb Mila, I carefully freed myself from under her arm and stood up. The room was in semi-darkness. Only the faint light of the streetlights was creeping through the slits in the curtains. I glanced at the sleeping girl, whose breathing was even and quiet, and cautiously made my way to the door. Gathering my things, I dressed silently, left the room, and headed for the car, where the driver was already waiting for me.

On the way home, I deliberately went over the details of the night in my head. I didn't want to admit that my sister was right, but it turned out that something new and unplanned to the smallest detail wasn't such a bad thing.

So today my sister and I are at the same place. My choice was a young girl, about twenty years old, maybe a little older. Unlike the first victim, she didn't stand out in any way, but I noticed an interesting detail on her arm — a green paper bracelet with a black print. The presence of this accessory indicated that the girl was at my friend's club last night. He sent me one of these along with the invitation. That set me up for an easy win. Entrance to this party cost a lot of money, and judging by the mediocrity of her clothes, this amount was impressive for her. Therefore, her desire to hang out in a crowd of wealthy young people was weighty, so it would be easy to negotiate with her.

Getting out of the car, I noticed a guy holding a takeaway coffee in a paper cup. Judging by the position of his hands, the coffee was already cold, which was perfect for me. For twenty euros, the guy kindly gave it to me. The plan in my head formed itself.

I smiled at my powers of observation and stepped forward confidently. The girl was sitting with her head tilted back and enjoying the sun. Her long, dark brown hair fluttered in the breeze. She wore a pink knit sweater, denim jeans, and white sneakers. She had a camera in her lap. It was my target for making contact.

Suddenly, she raised her head and looked around, which made me slow down. Taking my cell phone out of my pocket not to attract attention, I began to make an important call. I was only a couple of steps away from her.

As if by accident, I tripped over an invisible obstacle and flew straight at my target, and the entire contents of the paper cup spilled out onto her lap and the camera.

"Oh my God! What are you doing?"

The girl jumped up in utter confusion and stared at me.

"I apologize, I'm so sorry. I stumbled and lost my balance," I blurted out, making the most innocent face in the world.

"Oh no, not that," the stranger shakily tried to get the coffee-drenched equipment to turn back on.

"I'm sorry. Don't worry — I'll pay for the repair or buy the same new camera. It's my fault," I said, putting my hand on my chest.

She looked up at me, and suddenly I froze. A ray of sunlight had fallen on one of her eyes, and it turned light blue. The other was in shadow and was dark green. But as soon as the stranger's face was completely covered by the shadow, the iris changed and both eyes became the same color. It was mesmerizing and, for some reason, made a strong impression on me.

"No, it's not your fault. You didn't do it on purpose. It was just an unpleasant accident," the girl said softly.

The girl shook her head and did something I didn't expect — she smiled. And then a sense of unease crept up.

Chapter 4

(on behalf of Anna)

The guy was sputtering apologies, but all I could think about was what to say to my friend.

I certainly won't have the spare money to buy her a new camera now. I really hope I can get by with a repair, although that might be expensive too, I thought.

I didn't want to pass the debt on to the young man, even though he was persistent in offering to help.

"Anna, what the hell happened here?" literally squealed my friend, seeing how I tried to bring back to life her camera.

"Jules, just don't freak out. Sit down, close your eyes, count to ten, and take a deep breath. I'll explain everything. There was a little embarrassment."

I tried to speak in a measured voice, sitting her down on the rock.

In a nutshell, I described the situation. Of course, Jules' reaction was expected. And it was hard to blame her because she had been saving for this camera for six months, saving a considerable amount of money from each paycheck and denying herself many things. There was no reason to expect she would calmly accept everything and let the guy go without compensation.

"Okay, let him pay full price for the camera. We can look up the price online now. I get it. The man made a mistake, spilled the coffee, admitted guilt, and was willing to pay. I'm totally fine with that outcome," the friend concluded.

"I totally agree. Let's find a place to sit down, have a coffee, talk, and solve everything calmly," the culprit of the incident somehow confusedly suggested.

He must have been frightened by Julie's pressure, which was not surprising. She could discourage anyone with her directness.

"Jules, why don't we do this on our own?" I made one last attempt to save the guy.

"I'm glad you're so concerned about my finances, but believe me, these expenses won't hit my budget too hard," the young man said in a more confident tone.

His behavior seemed quite strange, but perhaps it was just a result of the situation. He looked like an attractive man, about thirty, but it was hard to tell for sure because the sunglasses hid part of his face. He had a strong build, an imposing stature, and a strong-willed chin. His pitch-black hair was neatly styled, only a few unruly strands disheveled and falling over his face. His smile was disarming, and his white teeth and plump lips could leave few people indifferent.

"In that case, there are plenty of places to eat and sit down. Take your pick, and I'll go buy a new pair of jeans. I don't really want to walk around with this stain," I said, taking off my sweater and tying it over my pants to hide the aftermath of what happened.

"Why don't we all go together?" the man suggested, rather unexpectedly, and then added, "In case you need an outside perspective."

"I think Anna can handle it on her own," my friend perked up and winked at me, letting me know that she liked this stranger, "and we could go to a nice cozy place and settle all the issues quietly."

Not wanting to be a third wheel, I went to get a new pair of pants, leaving them alone. The guy wanted to say something else, but Julia quickly took him in stride.

There was a shopping center near the square, where I found a reasonably budget store with a wide selection. Finding the right size, I hurried to pay for the purchase and changed my wet pair of jeans for a dry one. To my surprise, the new pair looked amazing, emphasizing all the best points of my figure.

Finished with the purchase, I headed for the exit from the complex. The only question was where to go. My friend clearly stated that her plans for the day had changed, and I didn't want to impose myself.

There was no desire to go home. The weather was still warm, and I wanted to enjoy it to my heart's content. Putting aside all sad thoughts, I confidently walked through the city streets I already loved.

Immersed in my thoughts, I didn't immediately notice the persistent phone ringing. When I fished it out of my bag, I saw Julie's number on the screen.

"Yes?"

"Anna, where are you?"

"Uh, I'm outside st. Peter's church. I thought you hinted that it would be better if I didn't come back."

"Look, Alex and I already worked it out. He's away on some business. But he offered to meet us tonight at a nightclub. What do you think about that?"

"It's not a bad idea, but I don't want to be a third wheel, and I can't get Max to go, you know that."

"Well, what does it mean to be a third wheel? Get rid of those thoughts! It's settled. We're going out tonight."

I couldn't resist Julie's pressure. But the truth is, I didn't put up much of a fight. It had been a long time since I'd had some fun, so it was time to fix that.

At the end of the conversation, We decided to go to her house, make ourselves fully prepared and get ready to have fun. All I had to do was call Max and let him know my plans.

"Hey, am I interrupting?"

"Not really. Everything okay?" My husband's voice clearly said that he was back to playing a computer game.

"Yeah, I just wanted to tell you I'm staying at Julie's tonight. We're going clubbing tonight, and I think we'll be back late. I'd rather stay at her place, so I don't wake you up and drive around town alone."

"That's a good idea. Have a good rest," my husband said and hung up the phone, deciding for both of us that the conversation was over.

This behavior was completely normal for him. Lately, our dialog had been kept to an absolute minimum.

After meeting with Julie, we went to the subway and got to our friend's home pretty quickly.

"Let's see, what should you wear tonight?" with excitement in her eyes, Jules went through the outfits.

Anderson took the initiative. She'd already fixed my makeup. And now she wanted to dress me in something, in her opinion, not boring.

I liked the makeup. Julie was good at it. But our tastes in clothes were very different. If I preferred smart casual, my friend loved more flashy and daring outfits.

"What did my clothes do to you?" I grumbled resentfully.

"Bored—that's one word for it. No offense, if you're going to work or going for a walk it's acceptable. But I'd like to add some brightness for a club party."

What a trendy girl," I grumbled to myself, but then I thought, "Maybe don't be a nuisance and try it on? As my grandmother says, he who does not take risks does not live life to the fullest.

After an hour of exploring the contents of the "style icon's" closet, we settled on a black tight-fitting jumpsuit and a metalized, thin mesh floor-length top that looked pretty good. I gathered my hair into a high ponytail, liberally dousing it all with hairspray. Earrings of silver color in the tone of the mesh were a great addition. All I had to do was pick out my shoes.

"Jules, these shoes should come with a guide to quickly identifying fractures," I said with my eyes rounded from the impression of the size of the stiletto heels.

As soon as I stood up, I felt that my feet did not obey me. They treacherously trembled at such a high altitude. In everyday life, I preferred more stable and comfortable shoes.

"Don't you know that? Beauty requires sacrifice. So bear with it, Cinderella," my friend summarized with a giggle.

While the fashionista was perfecting her hairstyle, I decided to take another look at the finished look. It was unusual to see myself in such an outfit, but the result was quite interesting. As I looked around, I noticed a green bracelet on my arm. It served as a pass to the club Alex had invited us to. This bracelet was left to me by one of my regular customers as a present for my last birthday. Yesterday, there was a great party with cool headliners, but I had an extra shift at the restaurant and couldn't go. After taking off my wristband, since it was a one-day pass, I wondered what today would be like with admission, hoping the price would be reasonable.

Fully prepared, we hailed a cab and drove to the other side of town.

"Listen, didn't this Alex seem weird to you?" I decided to ask.

"No. He seems like a great guy to me. Anyone else in his place would have just run away, and he paid for everything and organized the plans for the evening," she said calmly.

"I guess I was just imagining it," I shrugged and stared out the window.

Lights began to flare all over the city, drawing light lines and creating a cozy glow around. The evening sky was transformed by the rich colors of the sunset, painting the streets in soft shades of purple and deep blue. The shadows of the houses and trees casting silhouettes on the sidewalk added mystery to the atmosphere, and the light filtering through the foliage created playful reflections on the asphalt.

The half-opened window offered a mesmerizing view of this evening cityscape. Nestled comfortably in the seat, I savored this picture as if watching the world float by in the rhythm of city life. A light breeze blowing through the cabin brought pleasant smells of evening freshness, and the headlights of oncoming cars shimmered on the car floor, creating magical lights in motion.

Chapter 5

"Julie, where are you going? The end of the line is over there," I pointed in the opposite direction from the one my friend was pulling me through.

"We won't be in line today," Julie said conspiratorially and hurried along her intended route.

When we rounded the corner of the building, we found ourselves in a cozy alley lit by small lamps, where a door along the wall caught my attention.

"Alex said to be here by nine," my friend checked the time, "we are right on time."

A couple of minutes later, the door opened, and a skinny guy, about twenty-five, with a stunningly wide smile and the same color of hair as Julie's, fiery red, appeared.

"Are you Anna and Julie?" The guy asked and motioned with his hand to come in without waiting for an answer.

"It's us!" joyfully exclaimed my friend, and we went through the door.

"I am Alik, the right hand of the club owner. I was ordered to meet you and take you to the VIP box. Today, I will fulfill all your wishes."

The guy winked at us in a friendly way and led us down a dark maroon corridor filled with loud music rhythms and playful light flashes.

Another turn brought us to a neon-lit door. The assistant stopped before it and opened the door with a bright smile, letting us in.

"Come in," said Alik, shining with a snow-white smile,

"there is a bell on the table. Press it, and I'll appear."

We nodded, but the guy was already out the door, leaving us alone in a large room on the second floor. We could see the first floor through the glass, with a huge dance floor and a bar next to it. No music could be heard inside, just the vibration of the heavy bass. I noticed another door, with a staircase down to connect the two floors, and a pole in the middle of the room, probably for private shows.

Just as I was about to ask where Alex was, the door opened, and the waiters started bringing in appetizers and bottles one by one. Julie and I both opened our mouths in amazement. Following the waiters, a silhouette appeared in the doorway.

"Shall we begin our evening?" Asked Alex with his low and voluptuous voice.

"Alex, these are amazing. It's my first time in the VIP zone, and I couldn't even imagine how cool it is here," Julie said, glowing with happiness.

While Julie was having a pleasant conversation with the organizer of the evening, I couldn't take my eyes off the man. He wore loose-fitting jeans and a white shirt, tightly fitting his pumped-up body. Relief was easily visible through the thin material.

"Anna, is everything okay?" Alex asked smugly, bringing me back to reality.

"Yeah, everything's fine," I mumbled uncertainly, blushing.

"My friend will be joining us shortly. I hope you don't mind the company," Alex said and looked me straight in the eye, giving me goosebumps.

Julie and I shook our heads at the same time. Julie was excited and glowing, looking forward to the evening. I, on the other hand, didn't feel comfortable. Maybe the feeling that I was the third wheel didn't leave me.

My thoughts were interrupted when Alex decided to sit next to me. He sat down on the couch, pressing close to me. Our thighs touched, and like an electric shock, I bounced away, looking at him questioningly. I wanted to be outraged at the arrogance of it, but instead, I froze, staring into his light blue eyes, as clear as the sky. It seemed like you could drown and get lost in them.

Why is this guy causing such a storm of emotion in me? Ran through my mind.

"I apologize. I didn't mean to trespass. I slightly miscalculated the trajectory of my landing," the offender joked.

"It's okay, but I prefer to keep the distance," I said.

"I understand, and I promise to be more careful from now on," Alex said playfully, pressing his palm to his chest.

"Well, I'll forgive you for the first time," I replied with a smile.

For the next hour, I enjoyed the pleasant company. Alex and I chatted and joked merrily. Julia disappeared on the dance floor. And I wasn't even sure at what point or how long she was gone. The alcohol was also beginning to have its effect, bringing a sense of relaxation. Still, sometimes, I felt like Alex was mysteriously exploring me with his gaze. Noticing that his eyes were fixed on my neck and chest, a wave of warmth swept over me.

"So, you dream of opening your own makeup studio?" Clarified the interlocutor.

"Yes, and I think, in two years, it will be quite feasible. Working in a studio and restaurant, I can save a certain amount of money every month. So, every day, I am one step closer to my dream," I responded.

I started working only a year and a half after I arrived, as I had to settle all the paperwork and get a work permit. My first job was as a part-time waiter in a café near my home. It was a nice, cozy place with very nice owners. Later, when I was already familiar with almost all the regulars, one of the visitors recommended a salon where I could try to get a job. After a month of probation, I was floundering between two jobs, and although I was getting much more money at the salon, I didn't want to quit the café. All the staff and especially the owner couple were like family.

"And what if you had a chance," Alex hesitated a bit, his eyes fixed on mine, which made goosebumps scatter all over my body, "let's say, to get closer to your dream or to reach it many times faster?

"I would be happy, but I don't understand where you are going with this."

I looked at him questioningly and felt a lump in my throat.

His mood had changed dramatically. He became serious and thoughtful. All the fun had evaporated. I felt like I was looking at a different person.

"What are you ready to do for your dream?" Alex asked with a husky voice, reaching out his hand and gently touching my knee.

When I felt the warmth of his touch, I felt shivers all over my body. He fixed his darkened gaze on me and waited for a response. The rhythmic vibrations from the music's bass merged with the vibration of my heartbeat. I didn't want to believe what was happening. All those pleasant sensations that this man evoked dissolved in an instant, like morning fog before a sunny day.

How could he make such a crude and vile innuendo, even though it's not even an innuendo! I mentally resented him.

"I think you have misinterpreted my disposition toward you. If you heard my words as a call to apparently unacceptable actions, that's your problem."

I didn't wait for an answer. Adrenaline-fueled, I jumped up and headed for the exit.

"Anna, I didn't mean to hurt you. Wait, please. Listen to me."

Alex rushed after me, took me gently by the hand, and pulled me to him, but then he stepped back, maintaining a distance between us.

"Give me a couple of minutes, please. I really didn't mean to hurt you, and I can explain."

He was overwhelmed and confused. This made me more confused as I was completely unaware of what was going on.

"Okay, I'll listen. But honestly, I don't see the point."

This situation was absurd, but I became curious about what he could say.

Why listen to him? Just an ordinary wealthy guy who wanted to have fun, and that's all. What could he possibly have to say? And by agreeing to talk to him, I'm giving him hope, my inner voice tried to rouse my prudence. But I didn't want to listen to it. I wondered what Alex wanted to tell me.

We walked back into the room and found Julie in the company of a strange guy, laughing merrily and sipping a cocktail.

"Where did you guys disappear to?" She jokingly asked, "Look, we have a new addition."

"Good evening. You must be Anna? I'm Dan, the friend of the moody guy behind you," the new company member introduced himself, coming up to us and extending his hand, looking at Alex questioningly.

"It's nice to meet you," I shook his hand and walked over to my friend, who was already quite cheerful.

"Why are you looking so sad?" Juli asked me.

"Julia, would you be upset if I left?"

"Hey, what's wrong with you? I thought you guys were having fun. You were laughing so hard and shooting your eyes. I thought my legs would fall off dancing on the dance floor, but I didn't want to disturb you," Julie said in a half-whisper, looking at me worriedly.

While the guys were talking about something at the door, I told my friend everything that had happened.

"Well, he didn't say anything so terrible. Aren't you jumping to conclusions?"

"Are you serious right now?" I asked with rounded eyes.

"Anna, don't exaggerate. You're making a big deal out of it. We came here to relax, and he seemed to be just curious without forcing you to do anything. Don't be such a bore, please. Stop looking for problems where there aren't any. Take a break and enjoy the evening," she pulled me to her and hugged me tightly, "I'm here for you. If anything goes wrong, we'll run out of here together, blazing our heels. I promise."

"Ladies, are we interrupting?" Dan asked politely, approaching us.

"Not at all," Juli said playfully, winking at me.

Even though I still felt uncomfortable, I knew Julia was right. And the thought that she wouldn't leave me made me feel better. Besides, I'd promised myself a night of fun.

Chapter 6

(Alex)

Stepping out on the balcony, I deeply inhaled the aroma of the fresh night, feeling the soft touch of the light breeze on my face. Immersed in my musings, I lit a cigarette and gazed out into the endless lights of the night city.

How could I have made such a stupid mistake? Everything was going so well... I thought regretfully, gazing into the dark, endless space where the roofs of the houses merged with the night sky.

Anna was easy to contact, and there was a spark between us, but my haste crossed everything. Personal sympathy for this girl clouded my judgment. I wanted to possess her as soon as possible, drag her into Dan's office, and, without wasting a second, greedily sink my hands and lips into her body. In my mind, I imagined her moaning and arching from my touch, begging me not to stop, kissing me passionately back, and losing herself in my arms. These fantasies made my pants feel tight.

Lika seemed to have managed to arouse in me the interest and excitement of a boy. It's been a long time since I've lost my temper. But I must pull myself together, forget my attraction, and think more about the case. Nothing must stand in my way. The stakes are too high.

"I didn't know you were here," a quiet voice behind me snapped me out of my whirlwind of thoughts and brought me back to reality.

Turning around, I saw Anna. Her almond-shaped dark green eyes framed by fluffy eyelashes, her small nose, her plump, scarlet lips, everything about her was intoxicating and alluring. The warm light of the street lamp flooded the balcony, making the setting more intimate. But I promised to hold back and not give in to my feelings.

"I can't find the words to convey how sorry I am for my words. I'm just an idiot."

Over the conversation this evening, I could learn a lot about her. This girl had so much empathy and compassion for others that I had no choice but to take advantage of it. My mind was feverishly mulling over the next plan.

"I don't understand why you would even consider such an offer," she said reproachfully.

"My words were a pathetic attempt to achieve an important goal."

"Uh... Sex with me is an important goal for you?" The girl was surprised and looked at me with disbelief.

"Yes and no. But if you're ready to listen, I'll explain it."

I held out my hand to my companion, waiting for her decision. After a moment's hesitation, she gently placed her palm in mine. It was a pleasant sensation. And it was a good sign, which was more important. I had a chance to build trust. Anna followed me down the hall, and soon, we came to Dan's office where no one could disturb us. I knew the office well. I had been here countless times and had my key. Once inside, I took my time and let the girl look around.

The room was long but, at the same time, unusually cozy. The large floor-to-ceiling windows on the opposite side of the door filled the space with streetlights and gave the atmosphere a particular charm. Next to the windows stood an impressive desk with a computer and a mountain of papers. To the left of the desk was a massive oak cabinet that held important documents and a magnificent collection of vinyl records. On one of its center shelves was a rare gramophone, my gift to Dan for his thirtieth birthday. Opposite the closet, against the wall, was a soft sofa, inviting to relax, but even I didn't feel comfortable sitting on it, knowing how my close friend usually spent his leisure time with strangers from the club.

"It's a nice ambiance. But I don't feel comfortable staying with a man I don't know alone in a closed room," Anna was the first to break the silence and tried to speak calmly, but she failed to hide the worries in her voice.

"What I want to say should not touch the ears of outsiders, and there are many of them in this club. Please sit down."

For the next half hour, maybe more, I told Anna about my half-sister and our game.

As children, we often competed with her in everything — who could run to the playground edge faster or climb a tree higher? But every year, we grew older, and the game began to acquire new facets. Usually, we didn't involve other people in our rivalry, but as teenagers, we wanted something more interesting. When I was thirteen and Lika was sixteen, I encouraged her to seduce the most bullied guy in school and make him run around the school naked to prove his love. To my surprise, after this incident, the guy became the school star, and Lika was even in a relationship with him for a while. That time, for me, the whole story ended up losing my pocket money for three months, which only further atomized my excitement. With each subsequent game, the stakes increased, and the game tasks became more complicated.

And it was this childhood pastime that was able to pull me out of the hole. When, at seventeen, I lost my mother, the most beloved person in my life, I closed myself off from everyone and went into a deep depression. My sister, father, and stepmother took me in. But of all, only Lika did not give up hope in reaching and bringing me back to life for three long years. She tried every possible option, and one day she succeeded.

My sister's greatest asset was her gorgeous, long, white hair. She said she'd cut her head bald if I agreed to confirm my application to the university. I was full of confidence that she wouldn't keep her word, especially because she was due to have a wedding in a week. But that was a mistake. That day has been engraved in my memory for the rest of my life. After confirming the statement, I stared at my sister with a mute question, waiting for her reaction. Without a word, she took out an electric razor and began cutting off strand by strand. For a moment, I was speechless, seeing tears running down her cheeks as the blond curls continued to fall, one by one, to the floor. Realizing the full extent of what I had brought a dear person to, I felt unbearably hurt. Stopping her, I promised to learn and not to put a cross on my life.

Many years have passed since then. We, with Lika, distanced from each other, but the game was not abandoned.

I was struck by how attentively Anna listened to my story, not interrupting and empathizing. When I talked about my mom, I noticed how she clenched her hands into fists, biting her lips. It seemed to me that with all her might, Anna was restraining herself not to come to me. It was as if she could feel my pain and wanted to comfort me. But she managed to keep herself from such an impulse. The girl's openness and friendliness were very appealing.

I had to remind myself more than once what was at stake. "Del Rado" was the name of the winery I so desperately wanted to destroy. And not just burn it down but tear it apart and cancel all the contracts for the wine produced there, to destroy everything that had anything to do with the place. And despite my sympathy for the girl, it was crucial to remind myself that she was only a means to an end in the first place.

Her gentleness and responsiveness could play into my hands. Therefore, I presented my speech softly and pressed on pity by all means, trying to sleep Anna's vigilance. Having caught the right mood of the girl, I smoothly moved to business.

"This time, I refused to participate in the bet because I'm not a boy anymore, and I realize that things are going too far. But my sister found something to entice me," I paused, choosing the right words. "There is one place. It's very important to me and in Lika's possession. She took advantage of it and played it as a trump card, luring me into the game."

I briefly told Anna the essence of the bet, and in the process, I realized that this girl would never agree to sex for money, which would complicate matters and possibly lead me to defeat.

"After talking to you, I realized that I had made a mistake in my choice. Although I must say that I'm glad to have met you," I said carefully, as if walking through a minefield. "The sad thing is that I can't change my choice, and your refusal will hit me very hard. I could lose controlling interest in my own company. And this isn't about money. The company was built with sweat and blood. It's my brainchild. To lose my deciding vote would be as painful as parents giving their child up for adoption with the ability to only watch from afar but no right to influence the course of events."

"I need to digest everything... it's just too much..." she was confused, her words coming out hard.

My hope for the outcome I wanted began to grow stronger.

I managed to push pity, to hook her, but will it be enough? I thought.

"My intimate contact with you is simply impossible," the girl said cautiously, looking into my eyes. "I've been married for three years. And I've never cheated on my husband. I don't want to spoil the statistics," Anna joked strangely. This situation must have thrown her completely off balance.

My people had just started gathering information about the girl. Some of it was already on my phone, but I didn't have time to familiarize myself.

"I didn't know you were married," I admitted honestly, realizing that this news could complicate things. "Are you happily married?"

I tensed, staring intently at the girl's face, and was relieved to see the confusion. If she were happy, the answer would be obvious.

"Marriage, it's not easy... And that doesn't matter. My answer is unequivocal — no!" Anna replied sharply.

There was irritation and even anger in her. It was an indication that I had touched a sore spot.

Well, in that case, not all is lost, I thought.

Anna, quick on her feet, had already jumped up from her chair and headed toward the exit. But I couldn't let her go on that note. I made two quick steps up to her, took her hand, and turned Anna toward me.

(Anna)

In an instant, our faces were dangerously close to each other. Alex squeezed my hand gently, and I felt his breath on my lips. Waves of feelings and emotions swirled through me. Being so close to Alex confused my thoughts. I felt my heart start dancing, and my legs turned weak. My hands clung to the broad, strong shoulders of the man who had a strange power over me to keep me from falling.

"I know it's too much to ask, but just think it through. I'll give you anything you want," Alex whispered, so close that if I moved forward just a little, our lips could touch.

His breathing began to quicken. For every breath, Alex's powerful chest made contact with my breast. Without breaking eye contact, he slowly moved his hand to my waist and pulled me even tighter against him. A soft moan slipped from my lips, draining the air from my lungs, and I felt as if I were suffocating. The urge to give in to this temptation grew stronger and stronger.

But how am I going to live afterward? To give in to this attraction now would be to betray myself, my mind raced, and I clenched my eyes tightly as if I wanted to chase away a nightmare.

"I can't…" I whispered faintly.

"Then I'll have to keep my word. I promised I wouldn't violate your boundaries," Alex said with a wry smile and pulled away to get a business card out of his pocket. "My driver will take you wherever you want to go. And here's my number. Think it over and give me a call."

Chapter 7

After I got home, I couldn't stand it and told Julie everything. She got a few bottles of wine, and we spent the rest of the night drinking and talking.

Not very early in the morning, my head was heavy, either from the thoughts and emotions or from the alcohol. Of course, the latter was more likely, but the former shouldn't be discounted either.

"Are you awake? I made us some breakfast. It should help you get over your hangover easier," my friend chattered thoughtfully, putting a tray with orange juice, a couple of aspirin pills, and croissants on the bed.

"You're my hangover fairy," I thanked my savior with a

kiss on the cheek and began to devour the tray contents greedily.

"Listen, I wanted to ask you something," she began very gently. "You're my closest friend, and we talk about everything, as it seemed to me. I have had, and currently hold, absolutely no secrets from you. But only now have I realized that you always avoid the topic of your marriage. And I wonder why?"

"Jules, my head is splitting in two. Can we just put this conversation on hold?" I begged, feigning agony.

"Okay. Let's consider you left the topic again, but be warned, not for long. Now we'll rest, put ourselves back together, and go for a walk in the park. There, you'll tell me everything"

It seemed like a tempting idea to me to have breakfast, take a shower, and go for a walk. I waved my head vigorously in agreement and immediately regretted it. Every nod was a terrible pain. Julia giggled and stroked my sore head.

"Oh, you don't know how to drink. And I told you to drink a sorbent, and the morning won't be so cruel to you," my friend said, and went into the shower.

Finished with breakfast, I reached into my bag on the floor and pulled out my phone. As expected, there were no texts or calls. My husband probably hadn't even noticed my absence. As I was about to put the phone away, the home screen lit up with "Max", and the phone vibrated.

Hmm... maybe all is not yet lost for us, I thought in surprise.

"Hey, Max."

"Hey. When will you be home?" My husband asked worriedly, which made me feel uncomfortable. He's worried about me, and I didn't even think to call him.

"I don't know yet. I'm at Julie's right now. We were thinking of going for a walk to the park," before I could finish, Max interrupted me irritably.

"Anna, what park? Did you forget we promised to go to my parents' house for dinner today? And why are you at

Julie's? I thought you were on the night shift at your bar."

I was speechless for a moment. How could I think my husband cared about me? He didn't even know I worked at a cafe and not a bar where there simply weren't night shifts.

"I called you yesterday and told you I was staying with Julie."

"If you had called, I would have remembered," my husband said, still irritated. "You must have forgotten, and now you're making it up."

"Open your incoming calls and look. There was a call from me yesterday," my voice started to break from resentment.

"So? It doesn't say what exactly you said," he spat out with a sneer but immediately changed his tone to a calmer one. "Okay, it doesn't matter. You can come over now, and we'll go together, just like YOU promised my mom."

He specifically stated that it was my promise. Although, in fact, two weeks ago, he made me promise his mom that I'd come over to visit.

"Okay, I'll be there in an hour," I gave up because I didn't have much choice, and I didn't want to figure out over the phone.

"And one more thing. Buy some candy and a bottle of wine on the way. So as not to go empty-handed," my interlocutor quickly added and hung up.

Great, we're supposed to visit his parents, but I must buy the goodies. Although it's for the best. He would have bought the cheapest ones, and everyone would have eaten this crap all evening, I thought to myself.

After Julia, I took a quick shower. I struggled to make myself look more or less decent, briefly explained the situation to Julia, and rushed home, stopping at the store on the way. I got a text message from Max when I was in the driveway: "Meet me at my parents' house. I'll be waiting at Ben's."

My outrage was at an all-time high. Max couldn't even

wait for me to talk and walk around, just the two of us. From Julia's, it would be much closer for me to go directly to Max's parents and not make a giant detour.

Without going home, I headed straight to my parents-in-law's house, deciding to walk across the park. I needed time to calm down and not make a scene in front of strangers.

My heart ached at the thought of how long it had been since I'd seen my parents. It had been a whole year since I'd seen them. They came to visit for two weeks. My parents stayed with us. It was wonderful. I took a vacation, and we went out all day long. Max acted like a caring husband and blew the dust off me. The presence of my parents changed his behavior and attitude towards me.

I pulled out my phone and dialed my mom. After talking to my mom for about ten minutes, I felt much better. Dad's jokes in the background lifted my spirits, too. I didn't feel like complaining to them. I just needed to make sure they were okay.

When I reached the right house, I decided to do the same thing as my husband and texted him: "I'm here, meet me inside," put my phone away and knocked on the door. A minute later, I heard footsteps, and the door opened wide.

"My darling," Valerie Foster appeared smiling broadly from the door and rushed to embrace me, "Where is my son?"

"He'll be here in a minute. He decided to come to his friend to say hello."

"Then we'll wait for him inside. Come in. Dad is already waiting," Max's mom walked from the hallway to the dining room.

My husband showed up when we were all at the table. First, he said hello to his parents and gave something to his mom, turning his back to me. Afterward, he turned his attention to me, kissed me on the cheek, and sat down next to me as if nothing had happened.

Dinner was perfect, even though it was completely silent. Everyone was busy devouring the food. Valerie was a wizard in the kitchen. It always amazed me how Max didn't fatten his belly at these meals.

"Okay, kids. Now, before we serve dessert, I want to show you something."

Sighing heavily, the overweight mother-in-law climbed out from behind the table, and we walked toward the backyard. Before we reached the backyard, Mom stopped and turned to us.

"I always knew you were the best, but I never imagined I would receive such a gift," Valerie said, tears welling up in her eyes.

I gave Max a questioning look, as I had no idea what she was talking about. He just lowered his eyes and hurried out the door. I had no choice but to follow.

The courtyard looked marvelous. A month ago, it had been a shambles, with old tiles, a small vegetable garden between two almost withered trees, and a shriveled fence.

Now, there was new beige tile, a new wooden fence with a row of tui trees, a nice grill, and a neat little gazebo in the corner.

"It's amazing, how the yard has been transformed," it was very cozy and nice, but then I remembered her words of gratitude and decided to clarify, "Mom, what does this have to do with us?"

"Anna, have you forgotten what we talked about this morning?" Max looked at me meaningfully and turned to his parent. "Mom, Anna had a hard morning today. Don't mind her. She just forgot."

"Poor girl, she's been so busy with her work," Valerie shook her head and hugged me tightly. "Daddy and I are so happy to have such a wonderful daughter-in-law. Not everyone has a generous soul as you."

I stood staring at Max in utter bewilderment. He gestured to me, indicating that we would talk later, and taking his mom under his arm, Max headed toward the house. But I decided not to give him a chance to sneak away. I needed to find out everything here and now.

"Valerie, if you don't mind, Max and I will stay for a second. I'd really like to see the garden. We'll join you in five minutes," I said with a sweet smile, eyeing my husband.

"Of course, my darlings, I'll prepare the dessert," she said, and disappeared behind the door.

"What was your mom talking about? Why was she so grateful to us? And what were you talking to me about this morning?"

The rage was starting to build. My husband had obviously done something behind my back in his usual manner.

"Anna, first, calm down. Nothing terrible happened," my legal spouse said sharply but continued in a calmer way. "This morning, my mother dialed me, all in tears. You know, they took out a loan to fix up the yard. It's always been a dream of Mom's. But, there was a heavy rain at night, and the attic began to flood. The foreman came to them on an emergency basis, and during the inspection, it turned out that most of the roof was rotten and needed to be replaced. And all the money had gone to the yard, and no one would give them a new loan now. I didn't know what to do, so I consulted with Rene. And he suggested a good way out of the situation."

Max took me by the shoulders and stared at me with big gray eyes, clearly trying to push pity on me.

"I hope he advised you to take out a loan to help your parents," I asked, hoping for an affirmative answer.

Such an outcome of things would suit me. I would even help close this loan quickly, but knowing my husband, I had doubts. That is not a man who can solve problems on his own.

"A loan? Why? It would be difficult for me to repay it," my husband asked, being sincerely surprised.

"Where did you get the money from?" I asked in a

trembling voice, guessing what the answer would be.

"Anna, do you have no heart? Or have you forgotten how much our parents have done for us? If it weren't for them, you wouldn't even be here. How can you be so ungrateful?"

"Where did you get the money from, and how much?" Mentally saying goodbye to the dream, I repeated the question.

"Everything! Anna, I took all our money and gave it to my parents. This amount is enough for them to pay off the master as soon as possible to start work on the roof and sleep well. And I don't regret my decision for a second. Your fantasies about your studio are just dreams, and my parents' problem is here and now."

"Ours? In a year and a half, you've never helped me once! You're always asking me to give you extra money to buy something. And you laughed at me for denying myself everything and working non-stop," There were tears in my voice, despair, resentment, and powerlessness, everything merged into one. I looked at a man who was a stranger to me, "And you should live in the moment, or whatever you said? I wonder if I had followed your advice, what would you be doing now?"

"Ha, your petty nature has come out. What are you going to do? File for divorce? I don't think you're in a hurry to get back to your godforsaken town, and no one will keep you here without me. You should be kissing my parents' feet for pulling you out of your ass and showing you a good life," Max shouted in my face.

I wanted to object, to tell him everything I'd wanted to say for so long, but the tears were rolling down my face, and a lump rose to my throat. After years together, he didn't care about me or my feelings. He only saw me as something convenient for him.

Gathering the rest of my pride, I pushed away my assailant and hurried away, but he grabbed my arm and turned me around to face him, slapping me.

"Don't you dare behave like that in my parents' house! Wipe your tears and act normal, or I'll slap you again," Max yelled in a low voice.

My cheek was burning, my ears were ringing, and the ground was slipping away from under my feet. I couldn't believe this was happening to me. No one had ever laid a hand on me before.

Breaking free of my husband's clinging hands, I ran for the exit of the house. On the way, somewhere behind me, I heard Max's voice shouting something with a judging and threatening tone, and the voices of his parents, who didn't understand. But I didn't care anymore. All I cared about was getting as far away from here as possible.

Chapter 8

As I wandered through the city streets, I didn't notice that night had fallen. My eyes were swollen with tears, and my face was weathered. Turning down another street, I saw a public garden. It was lit by lanterns, but the shadows falling from the trees created unfriendly patterns and silhouettes. Shivering from the cold, I came to my senses and found that I had forgotten my bag with my phone and wallet in the house.

With no idea where I was or where to go, I felt panic coming on. Tears came to my eyes again. The easiest thing to do was to give in to the hysteria and fall to the ground, hug my knees, and start feeling sorry for myself. But common sense, which had returned in time, strongly advised against it.

First, I decided to look around and find the nearest subway. There, I would follow the signs to the center, and from there, knowing the way, I would go to my friend's house. The only problem would be meeting with the controllers since I didn't have my pass. But the fine bothered me much less than the probability of freezing in the street.

Wrapping myself in my coat, I tried to walk faster to keep warm. When I came to a wide street, I moved parallel to it, trying to find at least some familiar name on the signs, but alas, I had never been to this part of the city before. The entrance to the subway was nowhere to be seen.

After some more time wandering, I saw a gas station and had a new idea — to ask the employee to call me a cab and go to Julie's. Besides, I could stay warm inside the building while I waited. I was almost there when someone's voice called out to me.

"Anna?"

Turning around, I couldn't immediately recognize the stranger because the gas station lights were blinding my eyes.

"Do I know you?" I asked, confused.

"It's me, Dan. We met at the club last night," the guy said, a little embarrassed.

"Hi, I didn't recognize you," I honestly admitted.

"Are you all right?" The new acquaintance asked worriedly.

The young man came closer. Judging by his reaction, I didn't look my best. My feet were so cold that it hurt to stand, and I couldn't feel my hands. I was starting to feel very cold and tired.

"No, it's not okay, I'm lost and cold..." I said through gritted teeth.

Dan didn't wait for a detailed story and took me by the hand, led me to the car, sat me down, turned on the heater, and, closing my door, walked away.

My seat began to heat up, and warm air was blowing on my legs and arms. I warmed up fairly quickly and felt my eyelids become incredibly heavy. Unable to resist, I drifted into sleep.

Opening my eyes, I froze with shock. It seemed to be a

common occurrence for me to fall into a state of stupor these days.

I was in a spacious, light gray room with many windows and access to the balcony. A desk and chair stood in the corner, and a closet was built into the entire wall opposite the bed. All the room was designed in gray tones, and the furniture was arranged in strict geometry.

There was a quiet knock on the door. I pulled the blanket up over me and allowed entry.

"Hey, sleepyhead. How are you? How are you feeling?" My savior or kidnapper asked me courteously. It wasn't clear yet.

"Pretty good. I just don't remember how I got here."

With a cup of flavored coffee, Dan walked to the other side of the bed and sat down, holding out the drink. He looked different in the natural light than I remembered this guy from the club. His blond curls stuck out unruly, and his gray-blue eyes seemed startlingly bright and open. His broad forehead, straight nose, and light, thick eyebrows made his face very attractive, and his smile made me want to smile back. The guy had a very sturdy build. He wore a white T-shirt, emphasizing the relief on his arms, and light jeans. His whole image conveyed freshness and cleanliness.

"Yesterday, far past midnight, I was coming back from the club and met you at the gas station. You were frozen and exhausted. I thought you needed help. I didn't bother asking, put you in the car and went to get coffee. You were asleep when I got back," the blond guy said, shrugging his shoulders. "I didn't want to wake you up. So I brought you here and put you to bed in the guest room. I thought you'd wake up on the way to bed, but you slept very soundly."

"Thank you. You've been a big help, really. I don't even know how long I've been wandering the streets."

"Well, a true gentleman shouldn't leave a lady in distress," he winked at me. "Now drink your coffee before it gets cold and tell me what happened. Maybe there's something else I can do to help."

His smile was disarming, and it was impossible to contain all the emotional turmoil that had accumulated in me. I spoke, and he listened attentively, lying beside me and propping his head on his arm, absorbing every word. It was easy to talk. The words flowed out about all my hardships with my husband.

At one point, Dan rolled over onto his back and pulled me to him, laying me on his chest, stroking my hair, holding me close, and comforting me.

"I sympathize with you, but why in the name of God have you put up with this?" Exclaimed the guy when I finished my story.

"At the beginning of our relationship, he wasn't like this. We were very young when we started the relationship. But after we moved in together, he thought he had complete power over me, and it was like he went crazy. And our marriage was more out of necessity for a visa. If it wasn't for the circumstances, things could have turned out very differently. I think I succumbed to the pressure from both sides of our parents."

"Well, I still don't understand what his power is. He's not the Earth center, and your legal stay here can be arranged without his involvement. If that's what you want."

"I do now. Until two years ago, the only thing holding me back was his parents and the possibility of leaving my parents and stepping into the adulthood. I wanted to be independent."

I began to plunge into reflection on why it all came to be, and it became heavy on the heart, but the chance to divorce and free myself gave me hope for a better future.

"How can I apply for a residence permit?" I asked.

I was not familiar with the local legal system, and Max had always insisted that only the status of wife allowed me to be here.

"There are a lot of options," he smiled broadly again

and turned his head toward me. "The main thing is that you want to be here."

Being in bed with a stranger was surprisingly comfortable. Dan didn't cross the line. He often hugged me, but it was completely innocent. It was nice that he didn't try to take advantage of the situation but rather the opposite, trying to help as much as possible.

We lay in bed for quite a long time, talking non-stop, and all my tension vanished somewhere, and a sense of relief washed over my soul. Dan outlined the prospects of where I could go and where I could get help. I had already made up my mind to file for divorce as soon as possible and throw Max out of my life.

That moment was the starting point for the beginning of my new life.

For the next two weeks, I took a vacation. My employers stepped in and let me go. I didn't have much money because my husband had taken all my cash, but I had enough to buy at least food.

I had to fill in tons of paperwork, visit various authorities, and get the divorce proceedings underway. The amount of work ahead was daunting, but the spirit was determined, especially given the support from friends. Julie and Dan, who had become practically family over the days, helped me with the move. Although It was more like running away.

Choosing a day when my future ex-husband was not at home, we went into the apartment and started packing things into bags, throwing them into the car, and trying very hard not to attract the attention of vigilant neighbors. I didn't want to see my husband, so I had to act quickly and quietly, but the latter was a problem. Dan laughed and amused me and Julie, defusing the situation and preventing us from sinking into sad thoughts.

In the end, there wasn't a lot of stuff. Standing in the middle of the apartment, I looked at my former home last time. Only now, I realized what I had always missed so much. There was no coziness in the room. This house was as lifeless as my marriage to Max had been. It seemed like there should be some warm memories in a house we'd lived in, but they were all far away from here.

"It's going to be okay. We'll get through this," Julie whispered, hugging me tightly.

It was time to move on and take life into my own hands, no matter how scary it could be. I felt inside that something new, exciting, and tremendous awaited me. But if only I had known what life was preparing for me...

Chapter 9

(Alex)

"What the fuck? Why did you do that?" I was screaming at the top of my lungs at Dan.

I was filled with righteous anger. I'd been through a lot in my life. But I'd never expected betrayal from a friend who was like a brother to me.

"Maybe the problem is that I'm more human! And you starting to look more and more like a robot?"

"Who asked you to get involved? Everything was carefully planned. She'd have come to me on her own, and it would be a win-win. I'd solve her problems with being here and give her money. She wouldn't need anything. And what do you want with this unremarkable person? What's so special about her?"

"Do you hear what you're saying? First, she's a living person. You didn't see her that night. Anna was broken and lost, frozen through..." Dan paused and added calmly, "Lika is right. You created this company, successful and profitable. You put so much work into it. But you also put your whole soul here without a trace. You've lost yourself, man, and I'm sorry you don't realize that."

"I don't remember you thinking the same thing when you asked me to be one of your club's investors," I said, glaring at the man who had so skillfully twisted things in his favor.

"I've paid you back in full. I'm out of debt. And know what? I'm not going to give Anna to you. That girl is sweet, bright, and kind. Whatever you're up to, she'll be under my protection."

"I think I see what this is all about now. You've fallen in love," I guessed, not completely believing my assumption.

"Even if I did, it's none of your business."

"You know I won't back down, and I'll do anything. There's something more important at stake than a stupid crush," I said, my voice hoarse from screaming.

Dan and I had been best friends for a long time. I thought nothing and no one could come between us. But now I could see the contempt in his eyes for me.

"I may not have the power and opportunities you have, but I'm more like a human being than an emotionless machine," Dan said as he hurried out of my office, slamming the door loudly.

It was a low blow that I wasn't prepared for. I had just a week, and that wasn't enough time to make Anna do what I wanted. Thanks to Dan, things hadn't gone according to plan.

And I was one step away from winning, calculating everything I thought I could. While we stayed at the club, my people had compiled a complete background on her, her husband and his parents. The following morning, the perfect opportunity presented itself. His parents had a breakdown, not significant, of course, but a fake laborer was sent to the call, who quoted the required amount for his services. Afterward, for a small fee, a friend of Max's had persuaded him to take his wife's money and be a savior in the eyes of his parents. The only miscalculation was that Anna ran away without her cell phone. According to my plan, she was supposed to go to Julia who would definitely see me as the solution to all her problems, and everything could already be done. But instead, Dan got in her way and decided to play the role of a knight on a white horse.

No, it's my fault. I should have put a stakeout on Anna and shown up at the right moment instead of my friend. That sweet creature didn't deserve anything bad, but I had no choice. If I leave her alone, I have too much to lose. I need to reread the contract to make sure my actions don't violate it in any way. Also, it would be a good idea to get the experts involved and to get Dan out of the way. There's no time to waste. I thought and, pressing the selector button, addressed the secretary:

"Vicky, find Benjamin."

"Yes, Mr. Frai. Is there anything else?"

"Make two coffees."

Sitting tiredly in my chair, I pulled out the contract and reread the appendixes. About twenty minutes later, my head of security came in.

Benjamin was a sturdy man. He always calculated several steps ahead of his actions and had a long record of successful assignments.

"Ben, I have an important task. I can't trust anyone else. Take your best people. It is object number one, and here is object number two," I handed two folders to my subordinate. There was a complete background on Anna and Dan. "There are no financial restrictions. You can withdraw as much as you need from the card. The only limit is time."

"What exactly is the challenge?

(Anna)

I enjoyed my life at Julie's with all my heart. There were no rules, no sour faces, and no feeling that I had to adjust to anyone without end. In a word, freedom.

"Good morning, beauties," Dan said, flashing a white

smile, walking into the kitchen and putting the kettle on.

For the last three days, he'd been sleeping on our sofa. Julia rented a one-bedroom apartment three stops from the center, small, in a rather old building, but with good repairs and new furniture. Dan, on the other hand, had a large penthouse in one of the city's most prestigious neighborhoods. Why he stayed with us was not clear. Nevertheless, the guest did not cause discomfort for us but rather the opposite. Julia and I really enjoyed his company. So we didn't complain.

"Morning, sleepyhead. It's already the ninth hour, and I, unlike you vacationers, must go to work. So I'll leave you two in each other's care and run away."

Julia finished her coffee in one fell swoop and hurried out the door.

"Who's the vacationer? We're all back from the club at 3:00. But unlike you, I worked there and not flirting with the band," Dan tried to shout into the corridor, justifying himself.

Yesterday, Jules had a blast and spent the whole night chasing the frontman of the young but ambitious band. Poor guy tried to hide from her more than once, but nothing and no one could stop a drunk woman. I guess we'll be reminding her of that for some time to come.

In response to the guest's words, my friend appeared in the doorway, showed her opponent her tongue, and quickly rushed to work.

The salon was about three hundred meters from the house, but Julia managed to be late each time.

I took a big sip of my coffee and almost gave it back. It was bitter and awfully strong. Going to the cabinet, I pulled out a packet of sugar and tried in vain to pull out a pressed cube that was stuck and wouldn't budge. Suddenly, I felt Dan press his whole body against my back, gently run his fingertips from my shoulder to my hand, and deftly pull the sugar cube out of the packet.

"How many do you want?" He whispered in my ear.

I could feel his strong chest against my back.

"Two, please," I said, stammering.

Taking out another lump of sugar, Dan followed the second one into my cup, but he didn't move away. With each breath, his chest pressed me more and more against the countertop, and he kept his arms at both sides, encircling me in a ring. Confused, I just continued to stand there unmoving.

He ran the tip of his nose up my neck and captured my earlobe with his lips, giving in with his hips forward, pressing into me even harder, causing a wave of heat to run through my body. My body reacted to the movements, and I was afraid to lose my mind. In one motion, the blond tempter turned me toward him and clamped his hands firmly on my hips. Pulling me to him, he looked into my eyes and moved closer.

At that moment, I remembered the situation with Alex when we'd been alone in the cabinet, standing just as close to each other. But the emotions I'd felt then were nothing like what I felt now. My mind didn't even think about going into a fog. This whole situation was more perplexing than exciting.

I wanted to push Dan away, but he, in turn, abruptly covered my lips with a greedy kiss. With his left hand, he moved to my chest, his fingers pressing into my skin. My outrage picked up, and, taking his hand with difficulty, I could free myself.

"Dan, what was that?" I asked angrily.

I wanted to set things straight and explain that it was just friendship between us.

"I... I thought it was mutual," he said, and he pressed his hands against the countertop so hard that the veins in his arms swelled.

"There is reciprocity. But it's friendly and nothing more," I said calmly, trying to smooth over the awkwardness. "Look, this isn't a good time. It's too complicated..."

"Don't worry. I heard you. Friendly..." The guy repeated my words with a smirk and walked out of the kitchen.

A couple of minutes later, I heard the front door slam. A lump came to my throat. I didn't want to hurt Dan. He'd been a support and a pillar for me all this time. To say I didn't feel anything for him would be a lie, but I wasn't ready for a relationship right now.

As I replayed the last few weeks in my head, analyzing all the moments we'd spent together, trying to figure out if I'd given him hope for something more with my behavior, my thoughts were interrupted by a phone call.

"Anna, we are so screwed."

"Can I get a little more detail?" I asked tiredly.

"Yes, you can. I just left the salon. It's crowded and a mess. The tax inspectors came and made an inspection. Sabina managed to fire all those on the part-time job in one day so that they would not be fined because there were problems with the documents."

"I was sure her paperwork was perfect. And we were officially employed. I don't get it."

It was just morning, but I could tell it was supposed to be a busy day.

"Did you want her to tell everyone how she does her bookkeeping? And why do you think we make more money than other salons?" My friend was on the verge of a breakdown. "Anna, the rent is due at the end of the week, and under these conditions, as you know, the salary will not be tomorrow. Besides, I gave away my entire stash for the camera. We are officially broke."

"Wait. Let's not panic. I think I know how we can get out of this. At least partially."

My idea was to go to the café where I work and ask for an advance. It would be enough to pay at least half the rent. Moreover, we could arrange for Julie to take on a part-time job. With tips and a weekly paycheck, we would gather the remaining amount.

Wasting no time, I changed my clothes, called Helena, made an appointment, and my friend and I were there by eleven o'clock.

We sat with Helena Mair on the summer terrace. My boss was sixty-three years old. She had a short pixie cut, gray hair, light brown eyes, and a frail frame, but she was a very active and vigorous woman. She and her husband had owned Café Ekke for about fifteen years.

And today, I was in for another big surprise.

"This deal is like a lifeline for Thomas and me. Things hadn't been going well at the café for a long time," Helena said.

My eyes widened at those words; I was sure with so many customers, it was doing well.

"Don't look so surprised, Anna. My husband and I kept it quiet. We were hoping to raise prices, but we never did. We didn't want to downsize, either. Furthermore, we knew how hard it was to find work now, but we also knew we wouldn't last much longer. Thomas and I figured out that we could rent our apartment, move to Spain as we dreamed, and use the money from the deal to buy a small coffee shop on the waterfront."

Helen found these words hard to say. She was happy that her dream could come true, but it was hard for her to say goodbye, just as it was for me.

She told me that everything happened quickly. In just a week, a buyer had found a buyer and made a very generous offer, which was strange because the Ekke was not even for sale. But someone liked the place a lot.

"I'm happy that everything worked out for the best. You and your husband have always cared for everyone, and good things should happen to good people," I said with a smile.

"Thank you. I really appreciate your support. And what did you want to talk about?"

Julie wanted to say something, but I didn't let her.

"I have good news, too. Julie and I have decided to

take on a new, promising project, and I just wanted to tell you that I can't work for you anymore," I said, squinting at my friend.

"Yes, it's going to be an exciting project," Julie said playfully.

I didn't want to upset Helen and take my problems out on her, especially since she had enough of her own.

Chapter 10

In the evening, I talked with my parents and decided not to come back to their home at all costs. My parents are wonderful people, and I love them madly, but they always saw me only as a little child. If I go back, I'll be in their care. They've already mapped out my future years in advance, which means endless arguments.

"Why don't we call Dan? We're running out of options. No one's going to give us a loan that fast. And there's no money to pay it back yet. And we don't want to lose this apartment."

We've called every friend and acquaintance in the last couple days, but we've only managed to raise a fraction of what we need. Julie had a couple photo shoots booked. But they were canceled at the last minute. We tried to apply for jobs wherever we could, but we got rejection after rejection. In addition, my documents were being processed, but some of them were lost in the process of making new ones, and I urgently needed to make new ones, which meant time and additional expenses. It seemed like the whole world was against us.

"I called him, but he didn't answer. I guess he took a lot of offense."

"What a gentle guy. He's probably used to being able to get any girl he wants at the club. And then it was a bummer, and he just flew away like a wounded bird," Julie said and rolled her eyes.

"I don't even know what happened. He's been so sweet and helpful all this time, and then, one moment, it was like he has been replaced. I miss him a lot, but that's not our main problem. What are we supposed to do?"

"Anna, do you still have Alex's number?" As if casually, my friend asked, knowing full well that I, like her, had his number.

"What do you mean?" I asked with a raised eyebrow.

"Look, we both want to stay here. If he wanted me, we would be fine already. Just don't get worked up. I know you've got principles and all that, but you said he made your head spin. So why don't we at least consider it? If not, then no," Julie said in her usual tone, as if it would be easy to lie down under a strange man.

"I can't do it. I'm uncomfortable even thinking about it," I said heavily.

The thought of being a sex toy for money, even just once, made me feel like I'd been dipped in mud.

"I'm sorry. I feel sick for bringing it up. Forget it. Maybe we'll get lucky and figure something out in the last couple of days. Besides, tomorrow, Sarah, the receptionist from the salon, promised to send over a database of clients with numbers. Maybe there will be an opportunity to work out a deal with someone and get a part-time job. We won't make much, but it's better than nothing."

We spent the rest of the evening finishing porridge from some cereal found in Julie's kitchen and complete silence. We were each in our own thoughts. The only thing going through my head was that maybe I should really contact Alex. That would solve all the problems very quickly. He'd only called once since I'd seen him the last time, but I hadn't answered. It was strange that he'd talked so confidently about how important it all was, but he'd only called once. Perhaps he managed to resolve the betting issue differently.

When my friend went to her room to sleep, I took my

phone, found the contact, and looked at it for a while. Gathering all my courage into a fist, I typed a short text:

"Is your offer still valid?"

The answer came lightning fast:

"Yes."

"Is it possible to meet tomorrow and discuss everything?" I wrote with my hands trembling and immediately received a reply.

"Would it be convenient for you to drive up to my place in the morning? If yes, send me the address, and I'll send a car for you at nine o'clock."

I sent the address, and that was the end of the text messaging. A shiver ran through my body, and blood rushed into my ears. I was scared — what if I changed my mind at the last moment? Would he let me go? How would he behave? My mind was racing with so many thoughts, not happy ones, but pressured and frightening ones.

Climbing into bed, I curled up and wanted to cry, not understanding why my life had turned out this way. It took a long time to fall asleep, but eventually I did.

I convinced myself that it would just be a conversation, but just in case, I woke up early, showered, picked out an attractive outfit, and did my makeup. I was so nervous that I had to sit in the kitchen and look at the clock, waiting for the appointed time.

"What are you doing up so early?" Julie came into the kitchen, yawning and sleepy.

"I made an appointment to see Alex," I said, barely audibly, "But we're just going to talk to him first."

My first thought was to lie about my plans for the morning so my friend wouldn't talk me out of it, but after some thought, I decided to let her know. Since it was hard to predict how a meeting with a stranger would end, it was better if someone knew where I'd gone.

"Anna, are you sure? Have you thought about it?" The sleep was gone from Julie's face.

I just nodded affirmatively at her question, showing my unwavering determination.

"Okay. But leave me the address of the meeting and keep my number on speed dial. If anything goes wrong, call and run for your life."

"I don't have an address. A car will pick me up in half an hour," I replied in a shaky voice.

Julie's attitude made me panic.

"In that case, turn on your cell phone's internet. I'll watch your geolocation and try to be near you. And don't forget your speed dial. Also, try to look up the house number and text it to me," my friend said seriously.

This plan seemed reasonable, and my heart gradually returned to its usual rhythm.

"Do you think he could hurt me?" I asked.

"We don't know him or what he's capable of. It's better to be safe," Julia said and went to her room to get dressed.

She got ready as quickly as never before, and we went outside. Standing near the entrance and wrapped in my coat, I looked around, waiting for the car. The day was gray and gloomy. It was going to rain, and the wind was whipping through.

At two minutes to nine, a black Mercedes crossover pulled up. A driver in a suit stepped out of it, said hello, and opened the back door for me. My heart started to race out of rhythm again. After saying hello back, I cast a brief glance at my friend, who was standing on the other side of the yard and got into the car.

The driver turned his gaze to the road, started the vehicle, and we were on our way. I wanted to ask where we were going and how long the trip would take, but the words stuck in my throat. I took a couple of deep breaths, leaned back in the seat, and closed my eyes, letting fate take its course.

(Alex)

The morning was going to be at least interesting. Having canceled all the meetings for today, I paced back and forth in my cabinet, sketching out the options of events. Inside me, everything was boiling in anticipation of the upcoming meeting. It was hard to guess how the conversation would go. There was something elusive about this girl, something I couldn't predict.

"Mr. Frai, you have a visitor," Bennett's voice came from outside the door, breaking the flow of my thoughts.

"I'll be right down," I answered shortly.

That's odd. They're supposed to be here later. I wondered mentally and glanced at my watch again.

When I went downstairs, I found the uninvited guest.

"To what do I owe the honor?" I asked irritably.

"Are you out of your mind?" Lika decided to answer a question with a question.

"So, let's you immediately say all your claims. I'll pretend to hear you, and that's the end. I don't have time for more."

I had to get my sister out of here as soon as possible.

"Why did you put the girl through all this hell? You can't do things the honest way anymore, can you? And how could you do that to Dan?" Lika almost shouted.

"I'm sorry, but did I break the terms?" I asked calmly. She did not succeed in hurting me. "All means are good in war, you know that."

"Al, you can't do that. Anna's just a young girl. And Dan? He's your best friend. He's been there for you through the worst of it."

"Do you have the right to shame me? You know, you and Dan would make a great couple. Both of you are great at finding the speck in someone else's eye and not seeing the log in your own," I said irritably, as these champions of honesty and justice have already gotten on my nerves, "Perhaps I should remind you what you did to poor Kevin?"

"Don't you dare! I'm supposed to live with that burden

for the rest of my life. And that's exactly why I don't want you to live with it."

"Enough, Lika. To make it clear once and for all — I've grown up, and I'm capable of making and correcting my mistakes by myself," taking my sister under my arm, I led her to the exit, "Please, leave. I don't have time for you right now, really."

"I'll go, but please, before you do anything, look inside yourself. See how you will respond to your own actions," Lika looked at me with longing in her eyes and walked outside.

My sister always knew how to get through to me, and her look made my heart throb. I realized that I had gone too far. I had driven Anna to despair and sent my friend on a long journey.

I wonder what else I will be willing to do to get to the villa "Del Rado, I thought bitterly and went out after Lika.

"I'll try not to cross the line," I said calmly, and leaned over and kissed my sister on the forehead.

Chapter 11

The massive wrought iron gates slowly swung open, revealing a grand three-story house visible behind them. The snow-white walls contrasted with the gray-pointed roof, giving the impression of refined elegance. Huge windows adorned the facade, letting in soft light that invited them to explore every corner of the house.

The yard, like a work of art, was a magnificent extension of the stunning house. Everything about it was harmonious, from the perfectly mowed lawn to the whimsical shrubs lining up in bizarre shapes.

On the left side of the gate, I noticed a small brick structure, a little farther away from which there was a large aviary. I couldn't see its inhabitants, but considering its size, I could assume that the animals were not small.

In the very center of the yard was a beautiful fountain, around which there was a driveway.

On the veranda, in all his splendor, stood the owner of this house. Alex was dressed in a white shirt with rolled-up sleeves and black pants. He kept his hands in his pockets and his eyes on the Mercedes.

When the car parked, the driver hurriedly got out and headed for my door, but Alex held his palm up and stopped him, apparently to show his gallantry and do it instead of the guy. It all seemed unnecessary to me, and quickly pushing the handle, I opened the door. Alex reacted and offered me his hand, but I ignored it, trying to show that I didn't need that help. I put my foot out defiantly and deftly, unaided, jumped out of the car.

I wanted to put some boundaries between us. I wasn't happy about the whole situation, but Alex was clearly enjoying it, judging by the look on his satisfied face.

"Hey. I hope the trip was good," Alex asked with a

smile like a Cheshire cat.

"Hi. Let's leave the rules of good tone and get straight to the point," I answered in the most icy tone possible.

"I'd be happy to. My bedroom is on the second floor. We can go there right away," Alex said, raising his eyebrows and chuckling slightly as he gestured for me to follow him into the house.

His words made my legs shake and my head spin. But pulling myself together so as not to give him the joy of seeing the confusion on my face, I followed him confidently.

I wonder if that was a joke or if he meant what he said. On the other hand, that's the plan since the only way to save my and Julie's situation is through his bed. I thought as I paced behind Alex.

The inside of the house was just as stunning as the outside. We stopped in a large hallway near the front door. Opposite was a tall, wide staircase to the second floor.

"So, shall we go straight to the bedroom?" Alex asked, pointing to the stairs, "Or do we have a drink and talk about the details first?"

I could still hear the mockery in his voice.

"I'm glad I could cheer you up first thing in the morning," I answered grudgingly and added, "But I think I'll have coffee."

"In that case, let me take you to the kitchen."

I followed Alex. We turned into a long corridor, which was full of light even in bad weather because of the white walls and large windows. The whole atmosphere of the room seemed cozy and inviting, making me feel calmer.

Once in the kitchen, I experienced a new portion of aesthetic pleasure. The whole kitchen was Scandinavian style, white with a milky wood finish. The utensils were in light gray tones, the color of the apron. Cleanliness shone everywhere, and order reigned.

Alex walked over to the coffee machine, pulled out cups, and started making coffee. I sat on a high stool at the bar and watched the man.

"What kind of coffee do you prefer?" Alex asked in a casual tone.

"Cappuccino, if you don't mind," I answered and looked around, "A house of this size must require many people to maintain perfect order."

"It does, but most of them are off today. The only people in the house right now are Bennett, the house manager, and Grace, my cook, and just a wonderful woman."

"The house is perfect. At least the part I've seen," I said as I continued to admire the surrounding beauty.

"I had to work hard to buy it. There were many bidders for this residence. But I knew at first sight that I belonged here, and it's not my policy to give in."

"From what you've told me before, your determination simply knows no bounds."

"That's right. Now tell me, are you ready to state your terms?

Alex's sudden question brought me back to reality.

"Two thousand euros," I said my price quietly and uncertainly.

I lowered my head to hide my eyes from the shame that filled me and nervously began to fumble with the hem of my dress. It would be enough to pay rent and food for a month, and I'd have time to find a new job and get back on my feet.

"Is that your final price?" Alex's voice took on a more business-like tone, and all the joy and carelessness evaporated.

"Yes, it's enough for me," I answered without looking up.

Putting the drink on the table, he leaned toward me and asked calmly:

"You do realize this is a ridiculous sum for me and a heavy step for you, don't you?"

He leaned in so close that I could smell the scent of his perfume. It was enveloping, warm, and not too heavy, with cedar wood and spice notes.

"You asked for a price. That's my price. A larger amount won't make anything easier. And this money will go for the essentials and keep me from relaxing. I'll have to move on. And I'll have less time for self-abuse," I said quietly.

Alex looked at me in surprise and thought about something. He finished his coffee in one gulp, put the cups in the dishwasher, and walked over to me.

"Are you ready now? Or do you want to meet tonight?" He spoke dryly and looked past me.

For a moment, I thought we were discussing furniture shopping and nothing more. Not so long ago, such a cheerful Alex had changed into a real businessman without pity or compassion.

A lump stuck in my throat and began to squeeze painfully. Taking a deep breath, I gave myself a moment to think.

"Here and now," I answered, deciding to end it and not put it off.

"Are you sure?"

"Yes."

"Follow me," Alex said, still dryly.

(Alex)

I walked ahead of the almost lifeless Anna, convincing myself that this was nothing more than a deal that needed to be closed as soon as possible and not give myself a chance to change my mind.

We went up to the second floor and walked to my bedroom. I turned and looked at the pale girl pressing her whole body into the door. Sighing heavily, I stepped closer to her.

There was a reaction to my touch from her before. Maybe there will be now? I thought and moved closer to Anna.

With my fingertip I brushed her cheek, barely touching,

and tucked a loose strand of her hair behind her ear. Her dark hair beautifully set off her fair skin, so soft and delicate. I ran my thumb over her well-defined, plump lips, causing her to lift her eyes on me. And this time, they were a light green color. They darkened immediately after my touch, which meant I could arouse her desire.

"I really want to kiss you, but I won't do it against your will."

The girl froze at first. She was tense, but despite that, she leaned forward to meet my lips. With all possible tenderness, I kissed her, gradually penetrating my tongue deeper, caressing her, and gently nibbling her lower lip. My actions made her body shudder, letting me know that she was becoming more and more aroused. That, in turn, excited me, and I let my hands go free. Placing my left hand on her waist, I pressed Anna closer to me, and with my right hand, I caressed her neck and went lower to her breasts. Her swollen nipples protruded beneath the thin fabric of her dress. I squeezed one of them with my fingertips and twirled it, then immediately rubbed it, covering the whole breast with my palm, squeezing and releasing it. I enjoyed the girl's light moans, which she could not contain.

The desire grew stronger and stronger, and the kiss became hotter and hotter. I finally gave in to the feelings, lost all control, and picked up and sat her on my thighs. Her dress was pulled up, and I pressed the excited part of me into her crotch. A sweet moan escaped her lips straight into my mouth. My blood boiled, turning to lava and rushing through my veins.

Not wanting to delay any longer, I carried her toward the bed. I wanted her to be mine now. I wanted to enter her and feel the maximum intimacy, to possess her completely and get rid of this lust.

As I set the girl on her feet beside the bed and pulled away from her lips, I looked into her hazy eyes that were driving me insane. She was breathing heavily, gripped by as much desire as I was. But I needed to ensure she was willing to go all the way.

"Are you ready to continue?" I asked in a husky voice.

"No. I can't," she answered, panting, and pulled away, "I'm sorry, but it's too much. I thought I could. You pull me in like a magnet. My body goes mad for your touch, but it's a mistake. No amount of money is worth the loss of self-respect. I'd better go back to my parents' house. After all, it's not the end of my life. I can handle it."

Anna spoke nonstop, apparently voicing her thoughts aloud. At that moment, I looked at her and realized I couldn't let her go.

"Stop and take a deep breath. I promise not to do anything without your consent," I stared intently into her eyes and tried to speak calmly, but it was hard to regain my breath. "Please calm down. Get some water from the table over there by the window and breathe."

She looked at me apprehensively as if I would attack and tear her apart at any moment. I had to admit it was hard to restrain myself as my lust was at an all-time high.

The girl greedily clung to the bottle. Droplets of water flowed seductively down her lips and chin, over her neck, and down to her cleavage. She wore a black knit dress with a V-neckline that emphasized her breasts and hugged her stomach and thighs just below the knee. I imagined slender legs hiding behind the thin material, letting my imagination run wild.

"I need to take a shower, and then we'll talk. Make yourself at home," I summarized and headed for the shower.

It was impossible to think soberly in this state, and there was still the possibility that I would actually pounce on the poor creature.

Hopefully, the cold water will help me come to my senses. And if Anna decides to escape, she won't be able to. Not even a mouse can slip into this house without my permission. With those thoughts, I headed for the bathroom.

Chapter 12

(Anna).

Not taking a break from fighting my sudden thirst, I swept my gaze over Alex, who had gone to take a shower.

My heart tried to jump out of my chest, my lungs were short of air, and a shiver spread through my body. Even after a bottle of water, my mouth felt dry. And it was unclear what to do next.

He's clearly in no mood to let me go. And I wonder what we can talk about if I can't give him what he needs. I hope he doesn't take me by force. My mind raced frantically.

I wanted to text Julie but realized I'd left my purse in the kitchen. Leaving the bedroom, I walked down the stairs to the hall and followed the familiar path. My handbag was where I'd left it, along with my coat. Pulling out my phone, I saw ten missed calls from Julia and an impressive number of texts. Quickly dialing the number, I heard a worried voice:

"Are you okay?"

"Yes, I'm fine, but I couldn't," I said almost in a whisper and hesitated.

"It's okay. The main thing is that you're okay. Where are you now?"

"I'm still in the house. Alex went to take a shower and asked me to wait for him and talk to him."

"Why would he take a shower? Didn't you say you couldn't?" My friend asked in surprise.

"I don't know. He was nervous. Maybe the water calms him down?" I suggested.

"Okay, whatever. I think he will try to talk you into changing your mind, but if you've made up your mind — run away."

"I have definite doubts I'll be able to get out of here."

"Don't waste any time. While he's in the shower, go to

the exit," Julie commanded.

"Okay, I'll try. If I don't get out, I'll text you," I said and hung up.

I jogged quickly to the front door, making sure no one was around, pulled the handle, and walked out into the yard.

It was starting to rain outside, and the wind was picking up. Wrapped in my coat, I walked down to the road and suddenly heard a growl a meter away. I remembered the enclosures I had seen when I came here and their size. Freezing and without any sudden movements, I raised my head at the source of the sound and immediately regretted my decision to leave the house. In front of me stood a huge Doberman with a grin, and behind him, two more were slowly approaching. My whole life flashed before my eyes, and for a second, I was sad to realize how little I managed to do in it.

"Stop! Get back to your place!"

Alex's voice was so sharp and loud that I jumped on the spot.

The dogs flattened their ears and obediently followed the command.

"Thank you," I said, barely audibly.

"Let's go inside. A little more, and you'll get wet," surprisingly softly and with care, my savior said.

I turned around, and a new wave of shock hit me. Alex was standing there with only a towel tied around his hips, which was trying to slip off his oblique abdominal muscles. Raindrops fell on his firm chest, pumped torso, and strong arms. His black, wet hair fell over his incredibly handsome face. His bushy black eyebrows, blue eyes, chiseled cheekbones, and plump scarlet lips were maddening. Everything about this man was perfect.

No, I'd rather go back to the dogs. I'll definitely forget about principles and morals with this man. I told myself.

"I asked you to wait. When I came out and didn't see you in the room, I thought you'd run away. And precisely at that time the dogs are let out for a walk. So I didn't have a chance to get dressed," Alex informed me with a devilish grin as if apologizing for his look.

In fact, he enjoyed the way I looked at him shamelessly and blushing.

"I thought it was unnecessary to overstay my welcome," I snapped.

I'm sure it was a planned action. Alex came into the room like that, probably hoping to surprise me. I thought.

"Don't be silly. I'm glad to have you as a guest, and I hope you'll stay with me for a while," he said in a velvet voice and leaned down to pull me under the awning, "Shall we go back inside?"

My heart started dancing again, and the heat spread through my body despite the cold raindrops. Biting my lower lip bloody, I managed to pull away from Alex's seductive body, lower my eyes to the floor, and break free of his grip.

"Maybe I should just go after all?" I said quietly, not looking up at Alex.

"A brief conversation. That's all I'm asking," the guy in the towel said with a heavy sigh.

"Okay, have it your way. But I won't have any conversations until after you get dressed," I said and glanced briefly at Alex.

He nodded, smiled at me, and we walked into the house.

"Please go down this hallway. Second door on the left, and wait for me there. I'll be quick," the man said and hurried up the stairs.

Trying not to look at Alex's half-naked body, I followed the route and found myself in a spacious room.

The interior was in the style of the whole house - white and light beige colors. There were two gray sofas in a semicircle with a small coffee table between them in the center of the room. And on the left side of the door was an impressively sized bookcase.

The shelves were full of books in different languages of the world. I managed to find a complete collection of all the detectives by Agatha Christie, whom I simply adored. And every time I sat down to read a book, I couldn't tear myself away from it until the end of an obsessive desire to find out the name of the killer.

I was also struck by the sorting by genre, where each book was in its own section. And the authors were in alphabetical order, which was very convenient.

As I looked around more, I noticed a fireplace on the opposite wall from the closet, above which hung a portrait of a woman. It was hard to tell her age, not young, but not old, with black hair and blue eyes, just like Alex's. She also had very delicate features and a kind smile.

"This is my mom, Elizabeth. I hired an artist to paint a portrait of her from my favorite photo," came a voice behind me.

"She was a very beautiful woman," I said honestly.

"Yes, beautiful, but also kind, caring, and the best. I was lucky to have her but unlucky to lose her so soon."

I could tell by how he looked at her that he loved his mom very much, and the subject was painful for him. Longing and tenderness were reflected in his eyes as he looked at the portrait. I wanted to put my arms around Alex, hold him close, and tell him everything would be okay. But instead, I just looked at him sadly, sympathizing with his loss. It was hard to find the words in this situation.

"Did you have breakfast today?" Alex broke the silence first and decided to change the subject.

"Yes, a cup of coffee at home and then another cup of cappuccino that you made me."

"Great breakfast. It's called a quick way to gastritis," Alex shook his head, turned, and pressed the button on the wall.

A couple of minutes later, there was a knock at the door, and we were joined by a man in his sixties, with gray in his once-black hair, wearing a black suit and an amazing posture as if a metal pole ran through his entire body. He had slightly sunken eyes, a hooked nose, and very thin lips.

"Bennett, my guest, and I would like to eat. Can you have the covered patio ready for brunch and have Grace make my favorite pancakes?"

"Of course, Mr. Frai. Will there be any more orders?"

"No, that'll be all. Thank you."

The butler nodded and hurried away.

"Alex, what did you want to talk to me about?" I asked because my curiosity was driving me crazy.

"Let's sit down," Mr. Frai said, and we took opposite sides of the couch, keeping distance between us, for which I was very grateful, "According to the contract, if the girl refuses me intimacy, so as not to lose, I can offer her a six-month cohabitation. At the end of that time, she will receive a reward agreed upon in advance."

"That's an unexpected turn of events. Why didn't you say so before?" I asked in disbelief.

"I couldn't do it before you refused. That's one of the contract terms, or rather the addendum to the contract. And we don't just have to live in the same house as roommates. You have to be with me all day, except during work hours. I often work extra hours, but this contract requires me to be home by 6:00 at night. Or, in case of force majeure, you will come to me. Also, we have to sleep in the same bed, but without intimacy, unless you want more than that," he said with a glint in his eyes, and my breathing quickened.

The thought of being so close to him made my body tremble, and the room felt unbearably hot.

"And that's all?" I asked, confused.

"Not quite. My sister's confidant would still live with us to be sure we followed all the rules."

Alex spoke as if I had already agreed to all this.

"Is he going to sleep with us too?" I rounded my eyes and imagined in vivid colors such marvelous nights.

The thought made me laugh, as did the whole situation, which was already absurd to the extreme.

"No, the third will be unnecessary between us," Alex added with an undertone.

"It's too much, especially co-sleeping," I said, confused.

This point bothered me the most. After all, it turned out that if I couldn't stand the tension and gave in to temptation, it would be the same sex for money anyway.

"I must admit, this point is also the most difficult for me. I always sleep alone. No one should be in my bed if I need to get a good night's sleep," Alex said.

"Is there any way to remove this clause?"

"Alas, no. Lika added it on purpose, knowing that this was the point that could break me and allow her to win."

"It's hard not to note a "warm" relationship with your sister," I said sarcastically and smiled crookedly.

Our conversation was interrupted by a knock on the door. Bennett came to tell us that everything was ready for brunch.

"Come on, I'll feed you," Alex said affectionately and held his hand to me.

Chapter 13

We moved to the covered terrace, which looked more like a winter garden. Flowers in pots of different sizes decorated every corner. It made the overall atmosphere cozy and filled the air with marvelous scents. Huge windows stretching from floor to ceiling offered a mesmerizing view of nature. At the same time, the glazed roof took on the melodic beats of rain. Each drop tapped out its own rhythm. I wanted to linger in such a place, sit comfortably in a chair, and just enjoy the view.

"In these six months, will I be able to work?" I asked.

"I think it would be quite possible to set up an office in the house if you want. You'd just have to synchronize your office hours with mine."

"Can I ask for a private room? I'd like to have my own corner."

"Of course. I'll give you your own room, and you can even furnish it to your liking."

"I'm afraid I can't afford it. The most I can afford is to buy a shelf from Ikea," I replied, and I grinned bitterly at my situation.

"Don't think about money. During the whole period of your stay, you will be on my full support. Meals, shopping, hairdressing, and anything else you want are at my expense."

"It sounds tempting, but paying for food will be enough, and that's only until I start working. Then I'll be on my own."

"Anna, why sacrifice? You're not just doing me a favor. If we survive this period, I'll get something I never dreamed of. Think of it as an outside job that I'll pay you for."

"Look, this is kind of awkward," I said shakily.

"Anna, I'm taking six months of your life away from you. In return, I want to give you financial support and the opportunity to enjoy life, so to speak, as much as possible to brighten up your everyday life."

Inside, I already agreed to everything — to live in such an incredible house, on a complete board, and in the long run, to temporarily organize my office here. All in all, it sounded like a dream. Only the moment of our attraction to each other was still troubling me.

"Such an offer is hard to refuse. But promise to keep a distance between us," I said seriously.

"Do I have to?" Alex asked with childish naivety in his voice.

"Of course, it is. It's my condition. And for the time we

sleep together, I'll build a defensive wall of pillows between us. Promise not to break it."

"Okay, I promise to keep my distance. But just as long as you don't break it. And I'll try not to break the pillows, but I can't make a promise — I'm a restless sleeper," said the future neighbor, shrugging his shoulders.

What a sly fox. He knows how hard it is for me to stay close to him. And he's clearly up to something already. These six months will be a real challenge. I thought.

"In that case, it's worth a try."

"Does that mean you're okay with it?" Alex asked.

"I think so," I answered.

"In that case, I'll expect you with your things tomorrow morning. I'll bring my notary with the paperwork to make it official. Also, the contract will stipulate that if I violate your terms, you can leave anytime and get compensation."

"Tomorrow?" I asked in surprise.

"The sooner we start, the sooner we finish. What's the point of stalling?"

"I guess you're right. But what if I violate the terms and want to leave early?"

"You will not be penalized in any way. You must endure the entire term, but if it is difficult, you are a free person and can leave whenever you want."

"Am I right in thinking that I'm essentially risking nothing?" I decided to clarify.

"Exactly," Alex said and smiled.

"I have one last question," I paused to gather my courage before asking, "Is it possible for me to get an advance? I really need the money."

My face flushed. It was a shame to ask Alex for help, but if I solved my problems, Julie's situation was still critical.

"I believe we're talking about two grand. Do you want cash or a card transfer?" Alex asked softly, still smiling.

"Cash, please," I said, knowing that money can take up to three days to arrive by transfer, and my friend didn't have that much time to spare.

The manager brought us food, which was very timely. I didn't want to talk anymore because of the oppressive shame of my request. Alex attempted to break the silence, but I couldn't get over myself and pretend everything was fine. I didn't even want to make eye contact with him. He decided not to press, and after a late breakfast, we went to the exit.

"My driver will take you wherever you want to go now. And he'll be waiting for you at eight tomorrow," Alex said and opened the car door for me.

"In that case, I'll see you tomorrow," I said quietly, still unable to look at him.

"Have a good trip Anna."

The car drove away, but my future roommate stayed where he was, staring after the departing vehicle. For a second, I thought he was sad to let me go. Although, I probably just wished it to be like that.

"Is there a park nearby? Could we pick up another passenger?" I reached out to the driver after reading Julia' text.

"Sure, no problem."

After circling the park for a while, we found my secret agent. Julia managed to wait out the rain under a small awning without getting wet, but she was totally freezing.

We got home quickly. My friend was burning with curiosity the whole way, but I didn't want to talk in the presence of a stranger.

When we reached the driveway, we got out of the car and were about to say goodbye to the driver, but a man approached me and held out something.

"Mr. Frai wanted me to give this to you. Have a good day."

My friend and I nodded and hurried home.

The envelope contained money, the amount I'd asked for. Back at the apartment, Julie, despite her desire to know everything as soon as possible, ran to the shower to warm up. Then she joined me in the kitchen, where I made tea and told her what had happened.

"Listen, but you didn't give any receipts for that money. Maybe screw him. That guy got on your nerves. Let's say moral compensation, that's all. Let him deal with it himself."

My friend had developed a deep dislike for Alex for some reason. She urged me not to move in with him and to leave the money on any pretext.

"No, it wouldn't be fair. I made a decision, and I made a promise."

"He will put you in a cage for six months. And you'll just keep quiet and do whatever he wants you to do."

"All our agreements will be written in a contract and notarized. If he breaks them, I can walk away anytime and be compensated. I thought you'd be happier that at least you have money for rent."

"Really. I can't help but be happy. I've been given such a gift. Thank you, Anna."

After these words, my friend got up and went to her room.

I was left standing in the kitchen in complete bewilderment. What fly bit this girl, and why such a reaction? Finishing my tea, I wanted to cover my eyes for a second, but as soon as I did, he appeared in front of me.

Images of this morning popped into my head. I remembered his lips and the smell coming from his body, alluring and stupefying. My whole body was shaking at that moment, waves of heat spreading in my body. Everything inside me was aching with desire. His strong hands gripped my hips and my waist, making me moan with pleasure. I remembered the way my dress pulled upward and I felt the area around the zipper on his pants bulge. If he hadn't broken the kiss, I wouldn't have been able to suppress the desire.

But when he pulled away and looked me in the eye, I felt a deep dislike of self-loathing. I wanted him, really wanted him, but not for the money.

The phone on the table vibrated, snapping me out of my thoughts. It was a message from my mom. She wanted to know if I was okay.

I dialed her number and made up a story about finding a job and getting an advance. I told her everything was perfect and she had nothing to worry about. And at the same time I started to pack my things.

Chapter 14

I dreamed of Alex, or rather his eyes, in the night. They flashed brightly in front of me and vanished into thin air. I felt he was calling me, but I couldn't find him. I was running through a maze of some kind. Branches were sticking out of the hedge, clinging to my clothes, scratching my skin, and every step felt heavy as if my legs were filled with lead.

I woke up in a cold sweat, and for the first time, I couldn't catch my breath. It was fifteen to six, and there was no point in falling asleep. I went into the shower without much desire, hoping to refresh myself and at least cheer up a little after the strange dream.

Under the warm water, I managed to relax and put myself in a more positive frame of mind. Coming out of the bathroom, I checked my suitcases. Everything was packed, and I still had time to eat breakfast before the car arrived.

I paced around the kitchen, trying to decide whether to say goodbye to my friend or just leave. I didn't want to wake her up, not knowing what reaction I'd get.

"You wanted to run away without saying goodbye?" Julie's sleepy voice came from the doorway.

"No. I wanted to go wake you up, but I didn't dare," I admitted.

"Look. I said too much last night, and I'm sorry. I feel bad that I've never had an adventure like you have right now. From your story, it seems there's something between you and Alex, which means you have a chance to seduce such a rich and handsome man. I feel like I'm always out of luck."

"What are you talking about? Seduce? Don't be ridiculous. Imagine how many pretty girls are hunting him?"

He probably has his own army of model-looking girls who would do anything for a moment with him. I added to myself.

"Anna, you're driving him crazy. But be careful. I'm worried about you and a little jealous. And don't forget about me when you become the new owner of that fancy house."

We both laughed, and I hugged Julie tightly, vowing not to forget her and call her daily with a report. I don't know why she thought he was crazy about me, much less that I had any chance. I don't think that man is interested in anything but winning a bet. In everyday life, if he met me, he wouldn't pay attention.

My friend helped me carry my things downstairs, and an idea occurred to me as I got into the car.

"What if I tried to arrange for you to visit? Or maybe even work together like we used to. What do you think?"

"You should have started with that yesterday. Call me when you get a chance," Julie kissed me on the cheek and walked toward the driveway.

All the way, I went over everything I wanted to put in our contract, afraid I'd forgotten something important. I was scared but also excited about the whole thing. Somewhere in the back of my mind, I knew that I was attracted to this man. But I didn't know anything about him. It scared the hell out of me and added to my anxiety.

As the driver pulled the suitcases out of the car, I admired the house again and couldn't believe I was supposed to live here for the next six months.

The building was like a picture from a fairy tale. I couldn't wait to see all the rooms and the yard, but I had to remember that this was only temporary housing.

Bennett met me and led me into the house.

"Good morning, Miss Anna. May I take your coat, please? Mr. Frye is waiting. Follow me," the manager said quickly and clearly.

His diction was as impeccable as his posture.

"Good morning, thank you," I said, taking off my coat.

Bennett led me down a familiar corridor. While we were walking along, I had one question, and taking the opportunity, I decided to voice it.

"May I ask you a question?"

"Of course, Ms. Anna."

"Why do you address me as Miss and Alex as Mr. when, in Germany, we call them Frau and Herr?"

It was very strange to my ear to hear Miss and Mister. Although to be fair, it took me a long time to get used to Frau in my time.

"Mr. Frai has spent quite a long time in America. That's why he prefers to be addressed as Mr."

"And you? Are you from America?"

I kept pestering Bennett with questions, and he was not happy to accompany me.

"I was born in England," the manager replied briefly, and he quickened his step.

We passed the library I already knew and came to the door opposite. Bennett knocked, and when we were invited to enter, he opened the door and let me in.

The room was different from the ones I visited yesterday. Compared to them, it stood out in that it was extremely gloomy and seemed rather stern. It was a study with dark parquet flooring. The furniture was also made of dark wood, and even a large window did not change the atmosphere at all.

"Good morning," Alex said with warmth in his voice, walking over to me, pulling back a massive chair and inviting me to sit down. "Meet my notary, Gidon Heifetz. He's going to help us with the paperwork."

"Good morning. Nice to meet you."

I sat down and extended my hand to the new acquaintance sitting opposite me. Gidon responded with a soft handshake and a return greeting.

The notary looked to be a little over fifty years old. He had dark hair with a small bald spot in the front, a long hooked nose, small, dark brown eyes, and a thin build. But at the same time, his cordial smile was very disposing.

"I tried to describe everything briefly and clearly on the case without water. I think the lady should be given time to study the papers."

With these words, the notary handed me a folder.

Legal documents are not my speciality, but everything was written in simple and understandable language, even for me. The contract listed all the points we'd discussed yesterday, and Alex even added, as a must, the arrangement of one of the rooms as my office.

Another thing that caught my attention was the clause stating that during the period of cohabitation, I could take a week of vacation if I needed to take a break. This possibility pleased me very much. We were to spend the rest of our time together, except between nine in the morning and six in the evening on weekdays. I was also contractually obliged to have lunch with Alex. Breakfasts and dinners also had to be together and at least half an hour in length.

As I familiarized myself with the contract, it seemed like this would be easy to accomplish, especially after seeing what Frye had in store for me as a reward. He'd specified that I'd get some real estate and five hundred thousand euros. The final sum was never announced yesterday. I guess he decided for himself what kind of reward I deserved. It was a lot of money for me.

"Do you have any questions about the papers or wish to make any changes?" Alex spoke calmly with a sweet smile on his face.

"What kind of real estate are we talking about? We didn't talk about that yesterday."

"It's a gift from me, but you'll find out about it at the very end of the term. Are there any other questions?"

"No. I'm fine with it. You've put in everything we talked about and more. I think I'm ready to sign the contract if you're sure of the final sum because it's obviously overstated."

I tried to make my voice confident, but a slight trembling gave away my excitement.

"I won't change the amount. It's justified. And we don't need to hurry. I know I rushed things yesterday, but if you need time, we can wait."

Alex spoke very softly, and his voice acted as a sedative on me.

"Sooner we start, sooner we finish. What's the point of dragging it out?" I repeated what he said yesterday.

Whatever happens. Flashed through my head and I signed my name.

Mr. Frai signed next after me and Gidon sealed everything with his seal and final signature.

"Have a good day, everyone. As always, Mr. Frai, you are a pleasure to work with. I am always at your service in case of need," Heifetz said and shook hands with everyone and left us.

"Today is the beginning of our first day together, with which I congratulate us. Unfortunately, I will not be able to give you a tour of the house. I have to get to work as soon as possible. But you'll be able to lay out your things, settle in, and look around," the new neighbor told me, putting on a black jacket over a snow-white shirt.

Alex looked like he'd been born in the suit, very elegant and yet masculine. He wore a gray tie on his white shirt and interesting silver cufflinks on his wrists.

"It would be nice to know where my room was," I said sadly.

"Don't worry, Bennett will show you around. If you have any questions or requests, go straight to him," Alex said, and we headed for the exit. "I'm really sorry to leave you alone on the first day."

"Well, judging by the number of people working in the house, I'll be here, not alone."

I was uncomfortable staying without the owner of the house, but at the same time, it was clear that such a man had many things to do.

"Don't forget to be at my office by twelve," Alex looked at his watch and added, thinking, "No, it's better to be at my office at one o'clock for lunch. I can't promise I'll give you a hundred percent of my time, but I'll try my best."

I nodded, and Frai left the house quickly.

Chapter 15

Bennett showed me the way to my bedroom and quickly retreated. I guess he didn't like my company.

The room was cozy and carefully chosen: walls in warm colors made a pleasant impression, and the milky parquet added charm. A desk in the corner provided a secluded place to create and work. A little farther from the entrance, on the right side, was a large bed surrounded by bedside tables, handy for storing important little things. Opposite the bed were two doors. One led to the dressing room, where everything found its cozy shelter. The other led to the bathroom, promising moments of peace and relaxation. Spacious windows, letting in natural light, filled the room with light and freshness.

Having arranged everything compactly on a couple of shelves and a dozen hangers, I discovered that even shoes had their own separate place, as well as accessories. Everything had been thought out to the last detail, creating ultimate living comfort. With my modest supply of belongings, the walk-in closet remained more than half empty.

After finishing unpacking, I decided to give myself time to lounge on the bed. In recent years, I'd rarely had the luxury of just lying around in broad daylight. Sinking into the softness of the pillows, I savored the moment of tranquility, enjoying the picturesque view outside the window: green grass, branching trees casting shadows, and a lake of crystal clear water. But my contemplation of nature was disturbed by a knock at the door.

"Yes, come in," I answered.

"Miss Anna, your driver is waiting for you downstairs."

"Thank you, Bennett. I'll be right down."

Time flew by so fast. I said to myself.

I decided to wear my new favorite jeans, which fit perfectly, a beige oversized sweater that showed off one shoulder, and a quartz pendant around my neck that I'd never parted with. After fixing my makeup and messed hair, I hurried to the car.

Alex's office was in one of the tallest buildings in Munich, of which there were very few. I'd seen this building before, and when I saw it, I always associated it with an aquarium. The glass facade and curved architecture were probably to blame.

Once inside, I came across the reception and saw the chip card entry system. I didn't have such a pass, which confused me a bit. But my driver calmly walked forward and opened the way for us using his card. He walked me to the elevator, and we went up to the tenth floor and got right to the office.

"Hey, Vicky. How are you? I have a visitor and a request."

The guy said in an unexpectedly affectionate tone, addressing the secretary. At the same time, he did not drop a word on the road and was very serious.

"Hello, Jimmy. If you had come without a request, you

would have surprised me very much," Vicky playfully replied, but looking at me changed her tone to a sterner one. "Who's the visitor? Mr. Frai's schedule is second-by-second."

"This is my request. I need a pass. Ms. Anna will be a frequent visitor."

"No one gave me that order. Jimmy, I like you very much. But until Mr. Frai gives me a direct order. I can't do anything. I won't even let you into his office."

The girl looked at me coldly enough to make me look like I was nothing.

"Well, in that case, I'll wait here," I replied with a fake smile and settled on the sofa in the reception area.

Jim, was under the spell of the secretary and, forgetting about me, was whispering sweetly with her. The time on the clock was ten to one. I pulled my cell phone out of my purse and sent Alex a quick "I'm here" text, but there was no response.

An hour later, there was no change. I was still sitting there waiting for the same thing.

"Miss Anna, Vic's going to the dining room for lunch. I'd like to go with her, but I can't leave you alone. Would you like to join us?" Jimmy came to me when he realized I existed.

"I think I can handle this on my own. It's not that hard to just sit and wait. You can go to lunch now."

"I have direct orders to be with you out of the house, and I don't want to lose my job."

I don't recall any mention of babysitting in the contract. I'll have to take that up with the man who apparently forgot about our meeting and the contract. I mentally noted.

My stomach rumbled, and I didn't want to sit like a chain dog in the waiting room. Therefore, it was decided to go with the guys.

We went down to the first floor together. The dining room was located in the same building, on the opposite side of the entrance.

"Yay, my favorite table is still available."

With those words, Vicky led us to a table hidden behind a column and thus separated from the others.

We took our seats, and Jimmy, having clarified our preferences, went to get us food like a true gentleman.

"Miss Anna, what brings you to Mr.Frai?" The secretary asked me, and I could see the genuine interest in her gray eyes.

"You can just call me Ann. I came to see him about a personal matter," I answered briefly, not wanting to go into the details of our Santa Barbara.

"You were sent to replace Mia?" Vicky thawed a little towards me.

"No, who's Mia?" I was confused.

"No one," said the girl and became very nervous, which made me curious.

I couldn't think of anything better, so I lied to find out who Mia was.

"Sorry, I was just kidding. You're right. I was actually sent in as a substitute."

"Ugh, you scared me. I thought I had said too much," the secretary exhaled with relief. "What happened to your predecessor? She used to come two or sometimes three times a week, but now she's gone."

"She's sick," I tried to say with a nonchalant look, even though I didn't know what she was talking about.

"She hadn't been gone for three weeks, so what was she so sick about?"

"Flu with complications," I said the first thing that came to mind.

"Unfortunate one. I knew right away you were the replacement. I mean, who else would Jim accompany? I'm just surprised you got here at lunchtime. And you don't look much like Mia, or her predecessor Linda, for that matter," Vicky looked at me thoughtfully but immediately added. "Don't get me wrong. You're very pretty, but they usually send their girls in nice clothes, and the clothes are always brand name."

"I'm new at my job. And I haven't earned on a brand yet," I joked, trying to avoid details.

"Look, I didn't usually talk to the girls from the agency. You know, a lot of things to do, and there was no opportunity. But it was always terribly interesting, and how it is to work as an escort girl?" Vicky asked with genuine curiosity, but I was speechless after this information.

Luckily for me, Jimmy came back with the food and sat next to us.

"The schnitzel here is perfect, let's start. Bon appétit," Vicky hurried to change the subject when the guy appeared.

My appetite vanished, and the only question in my mind was why a man like Alex needed escort girls.

After we ate, we went back to the waiting room. I took out my phone and immersed myself in the Internet world. After another two hours of waiting, my lower back was aching, and my legs were stiff.

"Jim, can you take me home? I think I've consumed so much coffee, I feel like I could practically see time ticking away."

"I guess I can. I was ordered to be near you, so whatever you want."

The guy wasn't having fun, either. Vicky had a lot of calls and couldn't pay enough attention to him.

"Let's go home, then," I said tiredly.

I had a strong sense of resentment.

Alex forgot about me like I was some kind of thing. How is that even possible — to forget about a living person? Julie's right, that man is to be feared. I thought on the way back.

When I returned to the house, I went straight to my room and locked myself in, intending to sleep separately tonight. Since Mr. Frai didn't care about the terms of the agreement, I decided to follow his example. I spent the rest of the evening watching movies and fell asleep on one that wasn't the most interesting.

Chapter 16

In the morning, I was awakened by a persistent knock on the door.

"I'm asleep. Please go away," I replied sleepily and irritably.

My mood was the same as yesterday, not the brightest.

"Anna, I need to talk," Alex's voice came from behind the door.

What luck, he remembered about me. I said to myself.

"And I need to sleep," I mumbled and burrowed under the covers.

I heard the lock click and the sound of the handle coming down, and then the door opened with a distinctive creak. The uninvited guest slowly walked over to the bed and sat down on the other side of me. I was not going to leave my blanket shelter, but instead, I clutched the edges of the shelter tighter.

"I have no forgiveness for yesterday..." Frai started, but I didn't let him finish.

"You're absolutely right, no forgiveness. Now go away," I interrupted Alex.

"There was a misunderstanding. We signed the contract yesterday, but Lika's man could only arrive this morning, and without him, the days don't count. I had a lot of work to do. I got caught up in the moment and forgot to tell you. How can I make it up to you?"

He sounded guilty and remorseful, but his words didn't make me feel better.

"Yes, you're a busy man, but it was unpleasant and hurtful for me to sit there and wait, realizing that you'd just forgotten I existed," I said, still hiding under the blanket.

"I understand you perfectly well," Alex slowly but surely started pulling the blanket off, "That's why I wanted to find a way to fix it."

I didn't intend to surrender my fortification without a

fight, and I clutched tightly to the blanket, holding it with all my might.

"I object! You promised you wouldn't trespass," I shrieked as I felt that the fabric start to slip from my hands.

"There's no physical contact. I'm touching the fabric, not your skin, so it doesn't count," Alex laughed as he continued to break down my defenses.

A little more effort on his part and my fortress fell. I appeared in all my glory before him: swollen and without makeup, my hair disheveled, and my clothes were shorts and an old worn-out T-shirt. I covered my face and tried to huddle into a ball.

"Hey, don't hide," Alex said and added affectionately, "I want to see your face when I talk to you. Otherwise, I'll have to use force, breaking my promise."

After his words, there was no reaction from my side, and I continued to lie there, curled up in a ball.

Taking that as a call to action, he reached out his hands to my waist and started tickling me. Lucky for him, it was my weak spot, and laughing and wriggling, I struggled to get free. Bouncing on the bed, I jumped actually on top of him.

Facing him, I froze, staring into his eyes. Alex's pupils immediately dilated and darkened, and his hands slid down. Lifting my pelvis and grasping my hips, he dug his fingers firmly into them and pulled me into his arms, commanding and defiant. His movement was abrupt but pleasurable at the same time. In an instant, child's play changed into an irresistible passion and attraction between us. Even from light touches, both of us had a fire inside.

My nipples tensed and became very visible through the gray, thin fabric of my t-shirt. Alex lowered his gaze to them, moved over, and greedily bit down on the left one with his lips. A prolonged moan escaped me. As if in a fog, I tipped my head back, surrendering to the sensations and ecstasy of his proximity. I buried my hands in his black hair and pressed his head against my chest, giving him my consent to what was happening.

With one hand, he slowly moved from my hip upward, lifting my shirt and exposing my breasts. The other moved to my buttock and began to massage it hard. His breathing was becoming intermittent, and his gaze wild.

Alex licked his lips, and his tongue caressed the right nipple, uncovered, over and over again, touching the very tip, then circling the entire nipple. I squirmed as a wave of pleasure swept through my body. My crotch felt the swollen area of his fly, making me squirm in my seat. I was filled with lust and a fierce desire to feel him inside as soon as possible and end this sweet torture.

He pulled me down onto the bed, hovered over me, and put my hands behind my head, staring intently into my eyes.

"You have one last chance to say no. Otherwise, I won't be able to stop," he said, panting as he kept his gaze on me.

My body was aching with desire, and I wanted to say, "Do whatever your heart desires," but instead I said in a weak voice:

"No."

He let go of me and walked briskly to the door, paused for a second, and said without turning to me:

"I'll meet you downstairs for breakfast in fifteen minutes."

I sat on the edge of the bed and tried to realize what that had just been.

He has some extraordinary power over my body, but the remnants of my mind are thankfully still with me. It's a good thing Alex gave me the right to choose. On the other hand, it was detailed in the contract — intimacy by consent only, with a clear 'yes.' But at the same time, he could have kept going and just followed through. And after that, no one would ever know what happened between us. My mind raced at an unbelievable speed.

I showered, dressed quickly, and went to breakfast with

a clear intention to discuss everything and once again mark the boundaries of what was allowed on both sides.

Alex was already sitting at the dining room table, reading the newspaper. I sat down quietly next to him, trying not to attract attention because, at the sight of this man, all courage vanished and was replaced by universal shame.

A young girl in a governess's uniform brought our breakfast and hurried away.

"Why did you stop me?" Frai asked seriously but calmly, putting aside the paper and turning to me.

"You stopped yourself," I replied, a little surprised.

"That's not what I meant. You told me no. Even though your body screamed yes, wriggling beneath me, and your moans filled the room," Alex said in a low and voluptuous voice.

"It was just a moment of weakness, nothing more," I answered uncertainly, staring at my plate and starting to blush at the fresh memories.

"So it was just a moment of weakness," Alex repeated thoughtfully, running his hand under the table, finding my knee, and stroking it gently.

My heart reacted lightning fast to this action, dancing, and a new wave of heat swept through my body. But with all my willpower in my fist, I jerked my foot away.

"You and I need to learn to coexist together. This passion makes it difficult. Besides, if we sleep together, it'll be the same sex for money," I started in a confident voice, but the last phrase was barely audible.

"So here's the thing," Alex said, interlocking his fingers and directing his gaze towards me, "Let's look at this situation a little differently. Tell me, if you worked in a salon and there was a very handsome colleague, would he have a chance to have sex with you?"

"Hmmm... Workplace romances aren't the best idea, but it would have been a distinct possibility if I had been single at that time."

"Okay, now watch this. Your living in this house is actually a job for which you get paid. And I'm just a coworker because at the end of the day, I'm not empty-handed either."

"You're very clever at twisting the facts to your advantage. But tell me, what comes after?"

"Does there have to be an after? Why can't sex just be a good time with no consequences?"

"That suits you, but I'm not like that. Sex means more to me than just having a good time," I started to get peeve.

"And what does it mean to you?" Alex continued to talk calmly while my insides were buzzing.

I blushed, feeling like a schoolgirl who was called to the principal's office and tried to be accused of some misdemeanor. The last question cornered me. It would be too personal to answer, even though he'd seen my uncovered breasts five minutes ago, I had no intention of baring my soul to him.

"That's a question I don't want to answer. Maybe if you started talking to me as more than just a fuck object, I'd be willing to be more open with you," I said sharply.

I stood up and walked to my room without waiting for his response.

Chapter 17

Back in the bedroom, I pulled out my phone and decided to dial Julie. The screen showed about fifteen missed calls from her and even more messages. Dialing the number quickly, after a couple of beeps, I heard her worried voice.

"Hello, Anna, are you okay? Where are you?"

"Yes, I'm fine, I'm..."

"Why the hell didn't you answer the phone?" Julia was yelling so loud that my ears were ringing. "I was about to call the police. You haven't been in touch all day. I thought you'd been sold for organs or even something worse. We don't really know anything about this Alex guy."

Yesterday, I shamelessly canceled her calls because I didn't feel like talking to anyone.

"I'm sorry. Yesterday, like today, it was complicated. I'm sorry I didn't call back," I said guiltily.

"Can you go outside? I'm not far from the house now, as I've already prepared a plan to infiltrate and release you from the hostages."

"I need about five minutes to get ready, and I'll come out to you."

"Oh, that's great. We can go to the park, and you can tell me all about it."

I packed my bag and hurried to the exit. I really wanted to see my friend as soon as possible.

On my way out, I ran into Jimmy.

"Good morning, Ms. Anna," the driver said with a smile.

Seeing him reminded me that I had forgotten to talk to Frai about having a babysitter.

"Good morning, Jimmy. Are the dogs in the enclosure? And just call me Anna. We talked about this yesterday."

"Yes, in the enclosure. They only let the dogs out at lunchtime when you're not home."

"That's great."

As soon as I walked out the door, Jimmy followed me.

"Jim, thank you, but I'm going to the park to meet a friend, and I don't need any accompanying."

"I'm sorry, Ms. Anna, but I can't let you go alone. I'll get fired," my babysitter said, confused and guilty.

So what am I going to do with him? It won't be comfortable to talk in front of him, but I want to see my friend too. I mentally searched for options to solve the problem.

"Jim, do you know if I can invite guests?"

"Mr. Frai didn't say whether or not to let your friends in, so I guess you can," he said, scratching his head back.

Taking out my cell phone, I dialed Julie and suggested that instead of a walk in the park, we go out in the yard.

A short time later, my friend was already sighed and marveling at the beautiful house.

The weather outside was sunny and warm enough, so we decided to sit in the wooden gazebo in the backyard.

For the first twenty minutes after meeting Julie, I listened to what a terrible friend I was and how worried she was. Luckily for me, her tirade was interrupted by Bennett, who appeared out of what seemed like nowhere.

"Can I get you anything? Perhaps some tea or a light snack?"

"It's about time," my friend said without ceremony and put forward a whole list of requests.

Bennett didn't twitch a muscle in his face as he listened to Julie's demands. He politely asked us to wait and went to fulfill her request.

"What a service. Now I understand why you didn't call. Enjoying the moment," my friend winked at me, but I only grinned sourly in response.

I couldn't wait to share my experiences over the past few days. So I hurried to tell Julie everything that had happened yesterday and this morning.

"You're a real piece of work... " Julie said and laughed, "If I'd been mad at that jerk after your wait in the waiting room, I felt sorry for the guy now. You broke him so hard after you turned the poor guy on. And it's not the first time you've done it to him. I have to say, he's got nerves of steel."

"But that wouldn't be right," I hesitated, "We don't even know each other."

"Oh, yeah. Wrong, you say?" She smirked and shook her head, "Tell me, how old were you when you started dating Max?"

"I was fifteen," I answered quietly, not understanding what the question was about.

"You promised to tell me about your relationship. I

think now would be a good time to do it. And start from the beginning, please."

In my mind, I went back in time and began to tell about how I'd befriended a girl in my class named Kate when I was a kid. We spent all our time together, and she had an older brother, Max. He was pretty, short-tempered, had almost no friends, and rarely left the room.

When I grew up, and my body started to transform around the age of fifteen, my friend's brother started to show interest in me. He was only three years older than me, but when you're a teenager, that difference seems very big, and it seemed cool to show off a grown-up guy in front of my classmates. So, I gladly accepted his advances.

At the time when we just started dating, Max was sweet and kind to me, always met me at school, later, from the institute. He was my first and only boyfriend. But at some point, his family started having problems. Kate met a young man and ran away from home with him. No matter how hard they tried to get her back, they couldn't do anything. They just broke up with her completely. My friend disliked me, too, as I was no longer on her side.

On top of that, Max's father lost his job and couldn't find anything for a long time, and Valerie was dragging everything on her back as best she could, but at some point, she had a seizure. I came after Institut and tried to help with household chores. Max, in parallel with his studies, worked part-time wherever he could. And my parents tried to help financially as much as they could.

Valerie has a sister, and she and her husband found a way to immigrate to Germany. Half a year later, they arrived in the same way.

Valerie, with the support of my parents, insisted that Max and I get married so that I could travel with them on a marriage visa. The wedding itself was a mere formality, and it happened so quickly that I didn't even realize it.

When we settled in the new place, I hoped the bad things would be in the past. But, unfortunately, that didn't happen. Max had changed beyond recognition, especially his attitude toward me. He didn't care what I thought or did, where I was, or how I felt. His only concern was his personal comfort. And, of course, he never forgot to remind me that I owed him everything. Though it was not clear to me exactly what I owed him.

"It turns out that for almost eight years, you were an obedient daughter, a girlfriend, a devoted wife, and, of course, an exemplary daughter-in-law. In other words, you lived up to the expectations of the people around you. But here's a question: how happy did you feel in this correct world, where you had another's standards imposed on you?"

That question caught me off guard. After my breakup with Max, I felt incredibly relieved. I was literally relieved of a huge weight of responsibility. For the first time in a long time, I was only responsible for myself. I no longer needed to report to my parents or Max about where I was or what I was doing. I didn't have the headache of running home tired to make dinner and clean up. While I lived with Julia, we shared all the chores equally and did things not because we had to but solely by choice. I'm not talking about life in the mansion. It was like living in a resort. It was a new reality where I could live as I wanted.

With all these thoughts running through me, I finally felt free.

"I think you just had a realization," Julie said and smiled.

At that time, Bennett brought everything Julie had ordered and set the table.

"Can I still be of service?" The manager asked.

"No, that's enough. Thank you very much," I answered quickly, not giving my friend a chance to make a new order.

"Anna, you don't owe anyone anything," Julie returned to our conversation when the manager was out of sight, "And it's only when you truly realize that your life will begin to change. You don't owe me, Max, his family, or even Alex anything. You've been trained to help everyone and forget about yourself."

"Jules, I think you're exaggerating," I said with slight offense.

"We've been friends for three years, ever since you arrived. And I didn't even know what was going on in your family. You kept everything inside. But you always listened to the others and tried your best to help everyone. So, from now on, we're going to make you selfish."

"It sounds like fun," I said and smiled.

"And most importantly, it's good for the soul and psyche."

At these words, we laughed, and I suddenly felt very light at heart.

"You're absolutely right. Though it hurts to admit it, I really, for some reason, always want to be good and correct. And I don't want that anymore," I said, almost confident.

"You can't reset the factory settings in one day, of course," she said thoughtfully, "But you can already start adjusting. Maybe sex with Alex could help?"

"Oh, no. I'm not ready for that."

"Why not? Who's going to judge you?"

"It's not that. He just wants pleasure, no consequences, so to speak. For him, it's a kind of simple need fulfillment. I'm not like that."

"You want feelings?" Julie asked in surprise.

"I don't know," I admitted honestly, "But if Alex wants sex without commitment, he's free to go to his escort girls. I don't want to be his next one. And imagine what it would be like afterward. Living under the same roof for another six months."

"I think at this point you are right."

"And you know what annoys me most about him? He thinks he owns the world. And that he can get anything he wants at the snap of a finger. And he doesn't care about other people's feelings," the rebellious spirit that had been building up all these years woke up in me and directed solely at Alex. "It's time to teach him a lesson and show him that I'm a living person, and not a thing."

"That's my girl. I like your attitude," Julie said with a smirk.

The fire inside me began to flare up. It was fueled by the thought that I had lost a part of myself all this time. I became accommodating with everyone and trampled my self-respect.

The time with my friend flew by quickly. By half past twelve, Jim showed up and reminded me that we had to leave soon. We agreed that we'd give Julie a ride into town, but first, I decided to go to my room and change.

Searching through my clothes in vain, I couldn't find what I wanted, which was something sexy to tease Alex and escape. I liked the idea of teaching him a lesson more and more.

"Look, this is it," Julia said, handing me black pants and a red sleeveless blouse made of translucent fabric.

"Isn't that too fancy?" I wondered.

"Not if you don't wear a tank top under the blouse like you usually do," she said, winking at me.

Chapter 18

"Good afternoon. You must be Ms. Anna?" A new girl greeted me at the entrance to the office.

"Good afternoon. Where's Vicky?" Jimmy got very tense when he didn't see his sweetheart.

"Vicky doesn't work here anymore. My name is Elmira," the girl introduced herself in a friendly manner.

"Why was Vicky fired?" Jim and I asked almost simultaneously.

"I don't know," Elmira answered, a little confused.

At that time, a familiar voice sounded from the selector:

"Inform me as soon as Anna arrives," Alex said commandingly.

"Ms. Anna is already waiting."

"Let her come through."

Entering the cabinet, I felt as awkward and stupid as possible. About fifteen people were sitting at the table and staring at me. I think their attention was attracted by my lace bodice, which clearly showed my breasts under the thin blouse. Before entering the office, I took off my coat, expecting to impress Alex with my appearance but certainly not to stun all those people.

"Good afternoon," I said in a shaky voice and stared at Alex, wondering where to put myself.

"Anna," even the always steadfast Mr. Frai faltered, "Please come in and take a seat on the couch. We're in the middle of a very important meeting, and I can't move it. I'm sorry, but we'll have lunch together as we negotiate."

To say that I was surprised and taken aback was an understatement.

For the next hour, huddled on the couch, I sat with my lunchbox in my hands and shamefully covered my breasts.

I was not hungry at all, but only me. Alex, in his turn, was animatedly discussing future strategies of advertising campaigns, devouring his lunch and only occasionally throwing a guilty glance in my direction.

My first feeling was shame, and I immediately sank and shut down, even thought that I was to blame for the situation, as I dressed inappropriately and began to gnaw at myself. But by the end of the lunch, I remembered my friend's words and decided to look at everything from a different angle.

Alex could have postponed our meeting, warned me about the people present, appointed someone in charge for the time of negotiations instead of himself. There were many other options, but he chose the easiest and simplest. It showed once again how much he didn't care.

And as it turned out, when you stop blaming yourself, you can, quite quickly, develop a plan of revenge and possible variants of its fulfillment.

Feeling the fire inside me again, I squared my shoulders, proudly put my half-naked chest forward, stood up and walked right up to the man who spat on everyone.

"Can I go now?" I asked, looking at him languidly.

"Yeah, sure. But we'll finish soon, just twenty minutes, and I'll have a little break between meetings. I'd love it if you stayed late," Frai informed me, and his eyes began to darken.

In my head I interpreted his words as: *Don't go, I'll have a break soon, I'll fuck you, and then you'll be free.*

"Have a good day, Mr. Frye."

Turning around, I confidently left the office and headed for the car.

"Did you call Vicky?" As I got in the car, I asked a very downcast Jim.

"Yes, but she hasn't answered since last night. I thought she was busy as usual. But I guess the layoff got to her, and she's probably gone to her parents' house."

"I'm so sorry, Jim. When I get a chance, I'll try to talk to Alex. Maybe I can do something," I wanted to cheer the guy up.

"Thanks, but knowing Mr. Frai, I don't think you can change his mind."

Jimmy was right about that, but I wasn't planning on giving up either.

"Do you know if I can hire an assistant, for instance, at Mr. 'Stubborn's' expense?" I asked when it suddenly struck me how to kill two birds with one arrow.

"Mr. Frai said to make you as comfortable as possible, to spare no expense. He even set aside a separate account for that," Jimmy perked up when he caught my train of thought.

"Try to contact Vic and offer her to work for me, with all the same conditions, including salary."

"Will do, Miss Anna," my driver cheered up.

I didn't correct him about the "Ms. Anna" thing.

"Do you know how much is in this account?"

"I don't have the exact amount, but I know that the daily limit is twenty thousand euros. Mr. Frai warned that if the limit was exhausted, to contact him."

"What was Vicky's salary?"

"Three thousand, I think."

"In that case, we're not going home. We'll get a traveling companion and go to use the limit."

When I called Julie, all I had to do was say the magic word shopping, and she was ready for anything. I wasn't going to spend the entire amount Alex had allocated aside every day to punish him. For someone that rich, that would be nothing. But spending that money to torment him was much more exciting.

We attacked every major mall in the city. Julie bought everything she saw while I looked for the sexiest outfits, both lingerie and casual wear.

I intended to regularly bring Alex to the boiling point and leave him with nothing.

Upon returning home, my legs were incredibly buzzing with fatigue. Jim had been carrying things to my room in batches, and the number of updates amazed even me.

As I was about to go up the stairs to my room, Bennett called out to me.

"Miss Anna?"

"Yes?" I said tiredly.

"Mr. Frai expects you in the dining room."

"What time is it?"

"Six o'clock in the evening."

"Okay, thank you."

Oh, four hours of non-stop shopping went by fast. I wondered mentally.

Every step I took felt uncomfortable in my feet. As I

entered the dining room, I kicked off my shoes and sat at the table, ignoring Alex's presens.

"Did you have a productive day?" Frai asked as calmly as ever, making it clear that he didn't care how much I'd spent.

"Why did you fire Vicky?" I answered a question with a question, deciding not to beat around the bush.

"I'd always appreciated her diligence. I'd turned a blind eye to her weakness for gossip long enough, but she'd made an unforgivable mistake yesterday."

"Told me about your escort girls?" I asked straight away.

Frai hadn't expected such bluntness and raised his eyebrows upward in amazement.

Funny, I managed to surprise him. I mentally rejoiced.

"Vicky had a signed confidentiality contract, and she'd broken it. There's a giant fine under that contract, but I was limited to a consensual dismissal," Alex explained grudgingly.

"Consensual? That sounds more like pressure and a lack of choice," I objected.

"Well, she had a choice. Pay fifty thousand in fines and try to argue the dismissal in court," Alex said calmly, but it seems like he is not happy with all this stuff.

"To sue a big company and hope to win is pure utopia. You didn't give her a chance," I didn't back down.

"Why do you care so much about her fate?"

"I offered her a job as my assistant," without answering his question, I put Alex on the spot and froze, waiting for his reaction.

"Can I ask you not to do that?" still in a calm tone, my opponent asked.

"No, I need it for my maximum comfort for the next six months of living here," I replied just as calmly, matching him.

"It's just as unpleasant for me as it is for you when someone violates your boundaries. By working with Vicky, you'll violate my boundaries, which means I'll shamelessly violate yours."

"You already broke your promise this morning by not keeping your distance between us," I pointed out.

"And when you said distance, what did you mean, physical or emotional?" Alex asked with a sly smile.

It was stupid of me to doubt his cunning. He found a loophole here, too.

"I guess it doesn't matter anymore?"

"What if I make a new promise for physical distance and even talk it down to the centimeter, but in return, I ask you not to hire Vic?"

"My answer would be the same. Vic will work for me."

His honesty couldn't be relied upon. Even in this case, he could find a way around his promise.

"Well, in that case, the evening and night will be quite hot," Alex said, rubbing his hands together promisingly.

"Don't forget the condition. You can only penetrate me if I agree," I said the word penetrate slowly and sensually, and Alex clenched his hands tightly between them, making the veins swell.

"Your body throbbed with every touch I gave it. Do you think it would be hard for me to drive you crazy and make you moan and beg to come inside you?" He said in a low and sensual voice.

Even just his words made my throat tighten.

"And you know, you might be able to get me to that state and take advantage of the opportunity. But you'll never be able to make me truly yours," I said with a quick glance at the clock on my arm, making sure it was the end of dinner time and forgetting about my tired legs, I ran to my room.

I realized that I may have gone a little overboard in my games.

Chapter 19

Huddled against the door, I tried to catch my breath and regain my breath, feeling my heart pounding in my ears.

A couple of minutes later, someone started pounding on the door vigorously.

"Why did you leave in such a hurry? According to the schedule, we are supposed to spend some time together. So come out," my personal inquisitor said with a slight sneer in his voice.

"I thought you had a lot of work to do, and I didn't want to intrude."

"You'd be surprised, but I've rescheduled all my business for after nine o'clock. So I'm all yours for this evening," Alex said smugly.

"Sounds nice. I hope today, it's my turn to choose what we will do? I mean, it said "one by one". And since I'm your guest, you have to give in."

I was trying to stall for time in every way I could.

One of the clauses in the contract stipulated that every day after Alex's work, we should spend time on a shared activity, which we would take turns choosing.

"I can't say no to you. I'm all yours," he replied in a low, stirring voice.

"Okay. So I'll meet you downstairs in half an hour?" I asked with hope in my voice.

"I'm looking forward to it," Alex said with the same sneer, and I heard the sound of footsteps moving away.

I quickly pressed the call button on my phone and waited with bated breath for Bennett to answer.

"Yes, Ms. Anna, what can I do for you?"

"I really need your help. Please find two masseurs for a couple's massage. They should be here in half an hour. And if it's not too much trouble, please be here by then."

"I'll do my best," the manager replied with a dash of

surprise.

I need to hold out until nine o'clock this evening. And to keep Alex in line, I'll have to use Bennett. Since Alex is respectful of him, he won't allow himself to do anything impermissible in his presence. Feverishly, I pondered the next course of action.

Cautiously, I stepped away from the door and quickly headed for the shower. Once I was refreshed, I changed into a set of black lace lingerie and threw on a short, non-transparent robe.

If my plan fails, and I end up in Alex's hands, at least I'll look my best. I thought and glanced in the mirror before heading out into the hallway.

Walking down the stairs, I saw Mr. Frai and Bennett at the bottom.

"Bennett, you can be free for today," Alex shot his eyes at my feet as he tried to send out the manager.

"No. Stay, please. Did you fulfill my request?" I was having a hard time keeping my voice calm and confident.

"Yes, they're waiting for you in the salt room."

"Great, thank you for organizing this so quickly. May I ask you to accompany us and stay for the whole session in case we need anything?" I tried with all my might to keep the manager with us.

"Of course, Ms. Anna," Bennett answered calmly and walked forward.

We followed him.

Alex was completely bewildered, but he tried not to show it. He watched me carefully, without further ado.

I didn't even know about the salt room in this house, and I didn't even know what was in the others. I hadn't had time to look around in two days.

We came to the place, Bennett opened the door and let us in. The walls of the room were covered with white crystals, the floor was covered with sand, the ceiling was illuminated by diodes in a variety of colors, and the background music was pleasant and calm. Near one of the walls were three chaise lounges in folded form. In the center of the room were toweled massage tables where our masters were waiting for us.

After greeting the masters, I turned to face Alex and slowly threw off my robe, watching his reaction, but remembering we weren't alone, I grabbed a towel from a nearby recliner and quickly wrapped myself in it.

Frye swallowed nervously and began to remove his clothes just as slowly. Beneath the snow-white shirt was a thin, tight undershirt. The contrast of color making his velvet skin seem perfect. As he took off his undershirt as if to tease me, he began to play with his pecs. A devilish grin appeared on Alex's face. When he moved to the belt, I felt a wave of heat wash over my body. Reluctantly I turned away and climbed onto the massage table, lowering my face into the particular opening.

"My back will be covered, and you don't need to touch it," Alex gave instructions to his masseuse, clearly and distinctly.

I wonder why the back is not to be touched? How little I know about him, practically nothing. I thought.

I remembered seeing him in just a towel, but at that time, I didn't manage to inspect him from behind.

"Anna, next time, ask me for a massage. I'm pretty good at it, by the way," Frye said playfully from the next table.

"If I had that information before, I would have asked you. But as it turns out, I don't know anything about you," I replied just as playfully.

"Well, what would you like to know?" My neighbor asked seriously.

"Let's start with an easy one. What kind of music do you like?" Confused by this turn of events, I asked the first thing that came to mind.

During the whole massage, we talked very nicely. Alex calmly answered the questions, didn't evade, and seemed very relaxed, which surprised me even more. In music, we found a lot of shared preferences, as well as in cinematography. Our tastes, in many respects, coincided almost entirely. We even liked the same books.

We had a very heart-to-heart conversation at times, and the more we talked, the more Alex opened up.

"My favorite place, not far from us — in the Alps. The views and the air there are amazing. And in any season, there is something to do. By the way, do you know how to ski?" Alex asked.

"No. And I've never been able to go to the mountains. I just never had the time."

For three years, I planned to go to that area several times, but different circumstances changed my plans.

"Then it's decided. I'll check my schedule and take a couple of days to go together. I haven't been there myself for a long time."

In the conversation, Alex listed many of his favorite activities and hobbies, but it all came down to the fact that he hadn't done any of them for a long time because he was busy with work.

"Why do you work so much? There's obviously no vital need for it," I asked cautiously but rather bluntly.

"That's a good question, but I'm afraid I'd have a hard time answering it, even for myself," Frai said thoughtfully.

I had another question that had been on my mind since yesterday. I couldn't stand it any longer, so I voiced it.

"I also wanted to ask you about Mia. Why do you need the services of a girl like her? Don't think I'm being judgmental, just pure curiosity."

"It's simple and rather prosaic. I'm used to my day being on a schedule. And with girls like Mia, I don't have to waste my time. Meeting them is the perfect way to satisfy a physical need without making any effort."

His words made me feel uncomfortable. It sounded so cynical. It became clear why he had this attitude about sex. For Alex, it was really just fulfilling a natural need. But I couldn't understand why he was trying so hard to deny himself any opportunity to experience feelings and emotions. Although in our interactions with him, he wasn't callous and cold. And even this morning, at one point, he acted like a child when he tickled me and laughed. I couldn't quite put it all together in my head.

Each of us was absorbed in our own thoughts, and there was silence in the room.

"After the session, you should not get up sharply. Lie down for a couple of minutes and then slowly get up," my masseuse said softly.

"Yes, Anna, lie down. We can even stay here a little longer," Alex's voice had a playful tone again.

Back to reality and ignoring the masseur's words, I jumped up, put on my robe, and hurried out of the room.

It'll take Frai longer to get dressed, so I'll take advantage of the moment to run to my room. I thought as I went.

As I entered my bedroom, I pressed myself against the inside of the door and realized that I would have to go to his bedroom anyway, and there would be nowhere to run.

Going through all the options, I understood that I had only been able to delay the inevitable, and there was no further escape route.

He said he was still going to work after nine, and there's no one banging on the door. It means Frai is busy for a while. I need to call a friend. I thought, found my phone and dialed Julie's number.

When I heard her voice, I told her the situation. I hoped she'd have some wise advice.

"Look, if you need my permission, go ahead, friend, into the world of joy and pleasure."

"Julie, what does permission have to do with it?" I was genuinely surprised.

"Anna, all your decisions have led you to this situation. Which means you want it. You can deny it, but it's true. And your call to me is just another confirmation of that. You knew or at least guessed what I wanted to say, and you just wanted to hear it."

"Jules, I love you. But I think I hate you, too."

"I love you, too. And remember — this guy won't go

any further without being sure you're ready. Apparently, he's not an asshole."

"I hope you're right. Sweet dreams."

"I'm always right, and I wish you a really good night."

After talking to my friend, I went to the bathroom, washed off the oil, changed into my pajamas, and tentatively walked to Alex's bedroom. The closer I got to the bedroom, the faster my heart beat.

But to my surprise, Alex wasn't in the room. With a sigh of relief, I suddenly remembered about the pillow fort. With a quick step, I went to my room for building materials and began carefully erecting a defensive wall in the middle of the bed.

I hope he keeps at least one promise and really tries not to break it. I thought to myself, even though I knew it was foolish to count on it.

I grabbed my blanket, wrapped myself in it like a caterpillar, and fell asleep quickly.

Chapter 20

In front of my eyes was the same maze as last time. I ran and saw the same flashes with Alex's eyes. It seemed like I could find him just around the next corner. But it was all in vain. He was nowhere to be found.

The sun's rays filtered through the curtained windows and hit my face, making me squint and wake up. When I felt a heaviness in my chest, I thought it was the effects of a restless sleep. But when I tried to move, I realized that the heaviness was on a physical level.

When I opened my eyes, I immediately recognized the cause of my discomfort. Alex was brazenly resting his head on my chest, sleeping and snoring sweetly. At the same time, he was wrapping his huge arms around me tightly. His thick black hair was falling over his face, he seemed so sweet and defenseless at that moment.

I couldn't help myself and brushed a strand of hair away from his face, running my hand gently down his cheek, feeling the light stubble stabbing my fingers. At that moment, he was just mine.

Something made me think of Dan and the time we'd spent together. I remembered the strange kiss, after which he'd vanished without a trace. I stirred the memories again, trying to understand what he'd done and wondering if I'd ever see him again.

Staying in mental dialog with myself, I ran my hand through Alex's hair and began to finger it slowly.

"Good morning to you, too," Frai said with the look of a contented cat.

"Good morning. How did you sleep?"

"Surprisingly well. It was rare for someone to stay in my bed all night. I've always been uncomfortable having anyone around," Alex answered with a smile and still closed eyes.

"And when did you come?" I asked.

"About three o'clock in the morning. Initially, the plan was to wake you up and teach you a lesson, because you can't tease a hungry man with impunity. But you slept so sweetly that I changed my mind," he opened his eyes and raised his head.

"You're a real gentleman."

I tried to pull free, but Alex didn't even think about loosening his grip. Sparks flashing in his blue eyes and a playful smile appeared on his face.

His right hand served as his support and held me in place at the same time. Hovering over me, he drew his left hand from behind my back and ran his thumb over my lips, pulling the bottom lip slightly away, moving down to my chin, and stopping at my neck to look into my eyes.

"I'm going to drive you crazy," Mr. Frai promised hotly and continued his torture.

His hand slowly continued downward, his fingertips

sliding down my neck and moving to the hollow between my breasts. Then, finding a nipple protruding, he grasped it and squeezed it gently. The pleasure made me arch my back. He moved forward and kissed my lips. But he pulled away almost immediately. I froze, waiting for the familiar question, but instead, Alex smiled slyly and shifted his weight to the elbow of his left arm, pulled his right arm out from under me, and began to caress the inside of my thigh, spreading my legs slightly. My eyes widened with the unexpected, my breathing quickened, and my lungs were suddenly short of air.

Frye tilted his head toward my stomach, hooked my t-shirt with his teeth, and pulled it up. He froze for a moment, admiring my bare breasts with pleasure. His right hand slid gently up my thigh, moving to the most sensitive part of my body. The thin fabric of my pajama pants is not hiding the sensations.

Alex admired the view to his heart's content, lowered his head closer to me, scorching my skin with his hot breath, and greedily grabbed a nipple with his lips and pulled it inside, teasing the very tip with his tongue. At the same time, his whole hand covered my crotch, gently caressing and massaging it.

My moans echoed throughout the room. I arched up to meet his caresses and was lost at the moment. The pace of his hand's movements increased. I could feel my climax approaching.

"Are you ready for me?" Frai asked in a low hoarse voice, pulling away from my chest.

My mind was foggy, my head was spinning, and all I felt was desire, wild and unbelievably strong. Unable to verbally give a response no matter what, I shook my head negatively.

No, not right now. Not ready yet. My mind raced.

With my hand on his shoulder and the other firmly on the edge of the mattress. I was sure that at this moment, Alex would pull away and walk away. But he continued his rhythmic movements, biting my neck and kissing my lips hard.

When my body clenched with pleasure, and I moaned, he slowed his hand, gently stroking the throbbing part of me, letting me fully enjoy the release.

"I'm not that hard," Alex whispered in my ear, getting up and going to the bathroom.

My head was still spinning, and after catching my breath, I sat on the edge of the bed, wondering if he'd left for the shower in the same state I'd been in a minute ago. And even though he'd started it himself in hopes of ending things with sex, I felt uneasy.

Asking myself what I wanted right now, I quickly made a decision, took off my clothes and followed him.

Alex was standing with his arms and head against the wall under the water, his back to me. He hadn't heard me come in, and I had a chance to enjoy the sight.

The water ran down his hair, neck, massive back, exposed buttocks, and strong legs.

When I got within arm's length, I could see the thin, long scars in the center of his back. Everything clenched inside me. I remembered his instructions to the masseuse yesterday.

Frai started to turn, noticing me.

"No, stay there and don't move," I ordered.

To my surprise, he obeyed and turned back to the wall. I stepped closer and put my hands on the oblique muscles of his abdomen and felt his whole body tense.

"You don't owe me anything," Alex said, half-turned his head.

"I'm here because I want to be," I stood on tiptoes and whispered into his ear.

My lips gently pressed against his neck, nibbling, going down to his shoulder and back up. I put one hand on his belly and pressed my whole body against him, resting my breasts against his back; with the other hand, I slowly moved lower until I reached the hard, hot flesh.

I ran my fingertip from the base to the end, took the firm flesh in my hand, and moved it in a progressive motion. Frai clenched his jaw and tilted his head forward, surrendering to the sensations.

At the same time, I stroked his abs and chest. I loved to feel his muscle tension and caress his wet skin.

Alex let out a moan of pleasure, which was immediately echoed in my body with a new wave of heat.

"A little slower," Frai whispered, panting.

I slowed to his wishes, stretching out his pleasure. My lips continued to caress his back, neck, and shoulders.

His left hand covered mine on his chest, our fingers intertwined, clutching tightly. I could feel that he was at the peak of his arousal, and it made me even hotter. I bit his forearm in a burst of passion, and he let out a long moan and pressed the back of his head against me. His breathing quickened, and his whole body tensed and trembled, and I felt that he was finally able to release the tension that had built up in his body in one burst of ecstasy.

We stood immovably holding hands for a while longer as the warm water washed over our hot bodies.

"Can I ask you something?" I asked quietly, breaking the silence.

"About the scar on my back?" Alex guessed.

"Yes."

"I'll tell you everything, but not now."

Alex turned and kissed me gently on the lips.

He wanted to continue, but the loud rumbling in my stomach made him change his plan.

"I guess I'll have to feed you first before I can tease you again," Alex said, and reached for a towel.

We dressed up and went down to the dining room.

During breakfast, I remembered a few topics that I really wanted to discuss earlier.

"Why did you put a babysitter on me?" I asked.

"I'm afraid I'm not quite sure what that means," Alex

said with a raised eyebrow.

"Jim," I clarified.

"Oh, Jim. You don't like him?"

"He's a nice young man. But why would he accompany me?"

"It's for my calmness. And if you have any questions, you'll always have someone to turn to when I'm away," he said carefully.

"I'd like to be able to go out unaccompanied," I insisted.

"I have plenty of ill-wishers, and I can't let your safety be compromised," Frai said calmly.

I wanted to object, but Jim's presence didn't really bother me that much. And I wasn't in the mood for arguments.

"Okay, have it your way, but the matter isn't closed."

"You never cease to amaze me this morning," Alex said playfully and affectionately.

"Has that watcher, from your sister, arrived already?" I decided to change the conversation.

"Yes, yesterday."

"And where is he, and how does he watch that we stick to the rules?"

"He's at the guard post, watching the cameras," answered Alex.

Upon those words, I checked and erupted into a fit of coughing.

"Cameras?" I asked, still trying to clear my throat.

"Yes, they're installed all over the house. But before you panic, I want to reassure you. We don't have them in our bedrooms, toilets or bathrooms."

"It's great that you're just telling me this now," I said, shocked.

"The cameras aren't hidden. I thought you noticed them," Alex said with a smile, clearly amused by my reaction.

Looking around the room, I counted four CCTV

devices.

How marvelous to be as observant as I am. I noted to myself.

"But if there are no cameras in the bedrooms, how can he know if we're sleeping in the same bed?"

"There are sensors under my bed that detect pressure and movement," Frai said ordinarily.

"Based on this information, I'd like to make a statement. If we ever have sex, it won't be in your bed."

"To hear from you that it may happen is a great joy. And believe me, where it happens is the least of my worries."

Chapter 21

(Alex)

For the first time in a long time, I was driving to work, extremely reluctant. But I was warmed by the thought that pretty soon Anna would be coming over to my place for lunch.

I hated to admit it, but it seemed Lika was right again. Yesterday, during the conversation with Anna, I realized I had long ago stopped devoting time to anything other than work.

Besides, I was unrealistically excited by this game that was going on between Anna and me. I liked to pursue her, to push her slowly toward the cliff. But this girl was surprisingly resilient. I felt like a boy around her, impatient and eager for her attention. She'd even managed to wow me yesterday with her decision to hire Vic. It was evident she was just trying to mess with me, to prove something to me. But for how long she'd have the strength and passion, I wondered how quickly Anna would give up.

My thoughts were interrupted by a sudden phone call. And an unknown number popped up on the screen.

"Yes?" I answered the call.

"You're going to regret what you did."

"Dan, buddy, good to hear from you."

"I'm about to ruin your joy. And if you thought you could keep me here long enough, you were wrong," Dan said angrily.

"Look, you said you were tired and wanted to rest. As your best friend, I just wanted to help you with your vacation, that's all. Don't you feel bad in the Caribbean?" I asked with total calm in my voice.

"How's Anna? What did you do to her?"

That question made me pretty happy. Dan's memory wasn't always the best. And apparently, he didn't know Anna and Julie's numbers by heart. So he couldn't contact them.

"Oh, she's perfect. We'll be living together for the next six months, who knows, maybe more. I'm not sure if I can let that girl go. She's driving me crazy. She's got so much energy and desire..."

"Shut up. Don't you dare lay a finger on her. Or I'll kill you," his tone was almost shrill.

"I'm afraid you're too late. We had a very, shall we say, intense morning, bright and full of impressions."

"You'll regret it. You'll regret everything!"

The friend hung up the phone. His mind was always clouded with emotion.

I thought it would be good to assign Benjamin to check on Dan's vacation. His sudden appearance could really mess things up. He shouldn't be allowed to meet Anna. She's too impressionable, and if she knew the truth, she might take offense and give up everything in her heart. I couldn't keep Dan away from her indefinitely, either, so I had to take our relationship to the next level. The more this creature trusted me, the less chance of things going south.

The time before lunch was long. I only thought about my neighbor, wondering how this girl could capture my thoughts so easily.

I'm not allowed to fall in love with her. To enjoy this cohabitation is one thing, but to fall into the power of feelings would be unnecessary. I can't take that risk. I mentally reminded myself of my genuine objectives.

After waiting for a break in my schedule, I left the office and hurried to my car. I had a particular plan for lunch together today.

I was waiting for Anna to arrive at one of my favorite places in the city. It was a small but very cozy café with small tables, each decorated with fresh flowers, wooden chairs and soft cushions on top. The whole place was filled with the aromas of brewed coffee and fresh pastries. And calm, relaxing music played in the background.

It seemed that Anna would like this café and the pleasant atmosphere would put her in the right mood. The main task was to make her feel at ease and trust me. The situation with Dan was not pleasant, though his whereabouts were under control. It was hard to predict when he could escape. If I could tie Anna to me, there was a better chance she wouldn't decide to leave before the bet was over.

When Anna walked in, it was impossible to take my eyes off her. She had taken off her coat and was left in the soft pink dress that seductively tightened her figure. Her dark, long hair was loose, which contrasted with her fair skin, making her even more attractive.

"I hope I'm not late," Anna said.

"No, you're right on time," I said and took the top of her closet from her to hang on the rack, "You look wonderful."

"Thank you."

My banal compliment made a blush run down her face.

"This is the café I told you about."

"Does it serve apple pie that tastes like the one your mom used to make?" Anna asked.

"Yes. You have a good memory."

Is she so interested in me that she remembers such seemingly trivial things? I wondered mentally.

I carefully considered topics on which I could talk painlessly while giving the appearance of openness and rapprochement.

We placed the order, and Anna began to ask questions.

"I wanted to ask. Bennett told me you used to live in America. Why did you decide to move here?"

"I was taken to America after my mother died. My father, stepmother, and for some time already Lika lived there. After entering university, I had a business plan to set up my company, but the competition was too high in the local market. I continued my studies and collected statistical data about Munich. It was here that this niche was still free. Working alongside my studies, I accumulated a small amount of money and came here with it."

"How did you set up your company?"

"I had several options: to take money from my father or to do everything myself. Because I hate my parent with all my soul, I chose the second option," At the mention of my father, I involuntarily made a wry face. "So, for three years, I was beating the doorsteps of all investors, writing letters, and looking for meetings until I found an adventurer who dared to invest money. In five years, I was able to bring the company to a good profit and return the invested money with interest. Now, my creation is making multi-million dollar profits."

I was sure the next question would be about my father, but Anna pleasantly surprised me, perhaps sensing that I was uncomfortable with the subject.

"But what exactly do you do?"

"It's something like advertising, but we don't advertise products. Sometimes, we get orders, but rarely. In simple terms, we're in the business of people's reputations. We create the image of an angel or on demand we bring them to the bottom of the barrel."

"Aren't you afraid of a libel suit?" the girl's eyes widened.

"No, if you have the best team of lawyers in the state and keep a good detective. Sometimes, you dig a little deeper, and you can find a lot of skeletons in the closet."

"It sounds terrible."

"But it's in demand, and it's very lucrative. We do not work with ordinary people. Mostly, they are famous people in this or that field and believe me, they have many skeletons in their closets."

"I don't think I like it either way. But I'm not judging your choice either. Everyone goes their own way."

"Anna, I like how you look at the world around you. But it's a tough place. And the softer you are, the more painful reality can hit you."

"Why don't we make a little deal?" Anna asked.

"I think I'm starting to be a bad influence on you."

She looked at me, eyes wide open. This time, they were bluish-green in color. A sweet smile appeared on her plump lips.

"I'd like to suggest that you look at the world through each other's eyes."

"I don't really see how that's possible."

"We both love to read, but I think we understand the same work in different ways. What if I picked up some literature for us, and every night, we highlighted a special moment for each of us and explained why?"

I was amused by how this sweet creature tried to evoke kindness and gentleness in me. Her naivety seemed to know no bounds.

"I'm sorry, but that sounds incredibly boring. I think we can think of something much more exciting and energy-consuming to do," I said, and I had no trouble making Anna's face flush again.

Every time there was a dirty innuendo in my words, Anna bit the corner of her lower lip, blushed, and lowered her eyes shamefully. At such moments, I had a wild urge to pounce on her that I could hardly suppress.

I wonder if when I finally fuck her if this obsession will disappear. I think I'm starting to enjoy being infatuated by her. My mind raced.

"Good, then tell me what you plan for us tonight?"

"I haven't had time to work out for a few days now, so tonight, our schedule will be a little different. After work, you and I will go to water training, then dinner, and we can end the evening with a walk in the park."

"Water workout?" She asked worriedly.

"Yeah, in the pool. It would be inhumane to put you on strength training right away. Besides, water is good for endurance training."

"Of all the things you've listed so far, the only one that makes me happy is a walk in the park."

"You don't like the water?" I asked in surprise.

"I'm afraid," admitted the girl and swallowed nervously, "As a teenager, I once went swimming in the troubled sea. The storm got worse very quickly. I was sucked into the waves. I couldn't distinguish between the surface and the bottom. Struggling, I used up all my strength. I remember the feeling of helplessness and fear that came over me. I was lucky, my dad noticed in time that I went underwater and managed to run in and pull me out of the water."

There was a look of genuine fear on her face as she spoke, and it gave me an unpleasant tingle inside.

"I can promise you complete safety, and not just this evening. As long as you're with me, I'm responsible for you," I said seriously and added, "And you don't have to do anything you don't want to do."

"Thank you," Anna said quietly.

"By the way, I wanted to ask about the color of your eyes. Am I going crazy, or do they change color?" I voiced the question that had been tormenting me since our acquaintance.

"I have chameleon eyes. They change color depending on the light," the girl answered, embarrassed.

"I had never seen such a phenomenon before," I admitted honestly.

Chapter 22

(Anna)

I was coming back from lunch in a perfect mood. Alex was behaving differently, and I wanted to believe that our communication was beginning to change him, making him more sensual and open.

"No news from Vic?" I asked Jim when I got back to the mansion.

"No, her parents live in the suburbs of Berlin, but I don't have an exact address. General acquaintances don't know anything, either."

Jim was very depressed. During the absence of his beloved, he became very dark and withdrawn. I wanted to help, but I couldn't think of anything.

"We'll think of something, don't despair," I said

"Thank you," Jimmy said quietly and walked away.

The situation with Vic was strange. I didn't understand why she hadn't contacted Jim or even said goodbye.

Could Frai have had something to do with her disappearance? Maybe I should bring it up again tonight. I thought.

I spent the rest of the evening wandering around the house. I read, took naps, talked to every employee in the house, and even basked in the sun on the balcony.

There wasn't much time left until Alex arrived home, and I just remembered that I still hadn't picked out a swimsuit for practice. There were two of them in front of me, one sporty cut, no hints, the other the opposite, a dark orange bikini.

The longer I tried to choose, the more I realized that

the question wasn't about the swimsuit but what I was ready for tonight. Yesterday, I was ready to drive Frai crazy, but the more I got to know him, the harder I found it to fight my attraction to him. And I'm less and less willing to fight it.

Not without difficulty, I made my final decision, dressed, and headed to the training area.

The pool was not far from the winter garden. One part of it was indoors, and the other went outside, where the steam was rising in clouds because the water was heated.

Alex was already in the water, diving, and swimming for quite a while, which made me anxious.

I threw off my white robe, took off my flip-flops, and sat on the edge, sinking my feet into the warm water. I watched with pleasure as Alex's muscles tensed with his movements.

Noticing me, Frai once again dove in and headed in my direction. Swimming underwater, he spread my legs and came to the surface between them, folding his arms bossily over my legs.

"Why don't you come in?" Alex asked, wiping the drops off his face and returning his hand to my leg.

"I was admiring your skills," I answered with a smile, looking at my neighbor.

"Can I take your appearance as a direct provocation and a call to action?" Frai asked, looking down at my chest.

The thin fabric of the swimsuit could barely hide the outline of my breasts.

"There's nothing wrong with the way I look. You said there would be a training session, and I, being a responsible person, chose a swimsuit suitable for the occasion."

After all the agony of choosing, I was wearing a one-piece, unremarkable sports swimsuit.

"I have to admit, I was hoping to see less fabric on you," Alex said playfully and squeezed my thighs lightly.

"I think you'd be happy to see me without it at all," I played along.

"No, this is definitely a provocation."

After those words, Alex pulled himself up and kissed me greedily. But he pulled away pretty quickly.

"You're going to make me miss another training session. And I really need to stretch. So it's time to get wet," my neighbor said, pulling me into the water.

The next hour, Frai showed inhuman stamina and behaved like a responsible coach. He showed me exercises and held me at arm's length, which made me feel safe and secure. It was nice to know he fulfilled at least one of his promises.

"How are you feeling?" Alex asked after the exhausting exercise and wrapped me carefully in a robe.

"My legs feel weak, and my body feels weightless. I don't think I'll be enough for a walk in the park, and I'll probably miss dinner, too."

"It's a disappointing result, and we're going to have to work on your stamina," Frai said with his usual seriousness, and he picked me up and carried me to the exit.

"I'm tired, but I'm not that tired. Put me down," I protested.

"I'm sorry, but no. I need to conserve your strength."

"Or you could just put me in my crib and let me sleep," I said, yawning and snuggled tighter against Alex's chest.

"Sleep is mandatory in our program, but not now. Let's shower and have dinner first."

"Okay, coach."

"Good girl."

Alex kissed me on the top of my head and carried me into his bedroom.

"I thought I was going to take a shower at my place," I realized.

"The option of showering together is more interesting, and as your coach, I have to keep an eye on your condition."

Alex's eyes were playful.

There was no point in resisting, understanding perfectly well that if he had something in mind, he would definitely bring it to life.

We went into the bathroom. Alex put me on my feet, took off my robe, and started to take off my swimsuit. Slowly pulling off the still wet fabric, he ran his fingertips along my entire body, not missing the most sensitive parts of my skin. Every touch he gave me was accompanied by a gentle kiss. He gradually kneeled down in front of me. My skin went goosebumps, and my heartbeat quickened. Leaning against his sprawling shoulders, I pulled my legs free one at a time, leaving me naked.

Pulling the swimsuit aside, he put his hands on my hips, squeezed them with his strong hands, and dipped his lips to the indentation between my legs, caressing the skin on the inside of my thigh with his lips and slowly moving upward.

Arching my back against his soft lips, feeling his hot breath, I threw my head back and entwined my fingers in his hair. His caresses were so gentle and powerful at the same time that they drove me crazy and made me burn and die of desire.

Alex pulled away, looked at me with a hazy look, and asked with a hoarseness in his voice:

"Anna, I must understand. Are you ready to go all the way?"

"I'm not sure, but I don't want to stop," I answered honestly, panting.

Next to this man, I was losing my head, going crazy, experiencing sensations completely unfamiliar to me before. But every time, something stopped me. I didn't feel I was ready to say yes to him.

Wasting no time, seeing my exhaustion, desire, and sizzling passion, Frai buried his lips in me, caressing and teasing. He was everywhere, playing with me, bringing me to the edge, and then abruptly stopping, starting the torture all over again. I was barely on my feet anymore. I swayed, struggling to hold onto his shoulders, leaving red nail marks.

"Alex, please..." I screamed, begging him to stop the torture and let me finish.

He slowed for a moment. I thought Alex had decided to stop and leave me like this. But a second later, he suddenly moved his hand from my thigh closer to my crotch. While his tongue focused on the most sensitive area, his fingers penetrated me sharply, filling me and giving me incredibly pleasurable sensations. My moans increased as he quickened the tempo with his hand. I shuddered and clenched my whole body, my hands digging into his skin, enjoying the feeling of euphoria and the agony of ecstasy spreading through my body.

Alex held me up and helped me to stand on my feet.

"What was that just now?" I asked, trying to come to my senses in his arms.

"I wanted to give you a visual of what happens to me every time you deny me intimacy."

"It's not fair..." I whispered faintly.

"It's not fair the way you drive me crazy, the way you lure me in and leave me with nothing."

"In that case, take me here and now. If you only need my verbal consent, you have it," I replied with offense.

Alex didn't say anything in response but picked me up in his arms and carried me to the bed. My heart started beating a frantic rhythm again, and my head was spinning. I left the last of my strength in the bathroom under the onslaught of his own caresses. All he could get now was an exhausted body lying there like a log. Even my eyelids felt incredibly heavy.

He gently laid me in bed, covered me with a blanket, kissed me, and left. Sleep overwhelmed me almost immediately.

In the morning, my body was sore from the workout,

and my skin was terribly dry because I hadn't gotten in the shower that evening.

I was alone in bed. My roommate's spot was empty, which made me sad. I was still hurt by his words last night and the torture he had put me through. He wanted sex, and I wanted intimacy. I wanted feelings, not mere fulfillment of physical needs. And that was the main difference between us.

It was like a stopper in my head that kept me from moving forward without feeling reciprocated by him. But keeping him on a starvation ration wasn't an option either. I thought that if things continued like this, he might not be able to stand it and go to his escort girls to satisfy his hunger.

That thought immediately echoed a very unpleasant feeling inside. Even though it wasn't clear what kind of relationship we were in, I already knew for sure that I didn't want to share Alex with anyone.

Continuing to hover in my thoughts, I wandered towards the shower. Entering the bathroom, I found the cause of my anxious thoughts there. Frai was standing in front of the mirror, rubbing aftershave on his skin. He was wearing only a white, terrycloth robe.

"I won't let you miss any other workout. I'm not happy about your strength," Alex said in a casual tone, not taking his eyes off the process.

Without answering, I calmly approached him, turned him to face me, opened his robe, and knelt down. I wanted to give him a release, not by torturing him as he had done yesterday, but by being gentle and affectionate.

"Anna, you don't..."

"I know, but I want to," I interrupted Alex and continued.

Slowly, watching his reaction, I touched the foreskin, still relaxed, with my lips. Alex greedily and noisily sucked in the air with his nose. I took his dick base in my hands and slowly moved it back and forth. Pulling back the skin,

I exposed the head and ran the tip of my tongue around it. Opening my mouth, I covered his penis with my lips, kissing gently. Then I ran my tongue along the shaft, wetting it liberally with saliva. Frai closed his eyes and leaned against the wall, surrendering himself to my hands and moaning hoarsely.

Tilting my head back a little, I took the whole shaft in my mouth and began rhythmic movements, feeling the veins on his penis with my lips. I pulled in and pulled out the already hard and hot cock.

Alex was breathing loudly and heavily, thrusting his hips forward to meet my movements.

As I picked up the pace, I felt his whole body tense up.

"Anna, stop," he croaked, pulling away and cumming on the floor.

"Why did you do that? I wanted to finish what I started," I said resentfully.

It was a pleasure to watch his arousal during my caresses and to share his moments of ecstasy with him. I had never felt like this before.

Alex looked at me in amazement, came over, helped me up, and kissed me gently.

"Next time, I'll be under your complete command and no amateurishness, I promise," he said with a smile.

We stood in the shower, under the jets of warm water, soaping each other up, laughing and fooling around. Next to Alex, I didn't feel any shyness. I felt free and liberated. Although not so long ago, I was embarrassed to change clothes even in the presence of my own husband. Besides, Max never missed an opportunity to point out a flaw that made me feel unattractive. Whereas, around Alex, I felt like I was the most desirable and seductive woman in the world.

"Ready to go to breakfast?" Alex asked, wrapping me in a towel.

"I'm starving," I answered.

But we didn't want to leave the bedroom, so breakfast

was brought to us in bed.

While we ate, I decided to discuss something bugging me.

"Do you have Vicky's details? Her address or her parents' contacts?"

"Yes, I have a file on every employee. Why did you ask?" Alex asked calmly.

"Since she was fired, Vicky's been missing. They had some relationship with Jimmy, but he can't contact her."

"Maybe they weren't that close? I think she's upset about what happened and just took a break."

"Jim has been contacting her friends, but no one knows where she is now."

Alex reached for the phone on the nightstand and started calling someone.

"Benjamin, pull up Vicky Altero's info and find out where she is. As soon as you find out, let me know," Alex said in cellphone.

I didn't hear what person said on the other end of the line, but after saying goodbye to the caller, Frai turned to me and said:

"We'll know soon enough. Don't worry," he said and kissed me on the shoulder.

"Thank you. And do I understand correctly that you're already okay with me hiring her?" I asked incredulously.

"I'm still against it, but I can't influence your decision. So, I just have to accept it," Alex answered and shrugged.

"I'll mark this day in red on my calendar. Did Mr. Frai surrender without a fight?" I said, not believing what was happening.

"In a way, you surrendered too. So the taste of defeat isn't so bad," my neighbor replied with a devilish grin.

Chapter 23

The following month was heaven on earth. Alex opened up from new sides, and every day, he let me get closer to him, as I did to him.

In the evenings, we practiced together, went for walks, went to a club, and took painting lessons, which, by the way, was a complete failure, but we laughed for a long time, and afterward, we washed off the paint from our dirty bodies with particular pleasure. On weekends, we would have a movie marathon or go camping.

My roommate even helped me set up my office. The workroom was even better than I had imagined in my fantasies. There was a comfortable dresser with a mirror, perfect lighting, many cabinets, and a completely updated set of cosmetics.

The size of my office allowed me to design a corner for photo shoots, where Julie often hung out, bringing her paraphernalia. We turned out to be a marvelous tandem, with me doing the makeup and my friend doing the photo shoot.

Things with Alex remained the same as before. There were always sparks flying between us, and there was passion, but I couldn't make up my mind to say yes to him. He sensed my uncertainty and didn't push anymore, kept waiting, and didn't try to torment me about it. I still lacked in his actions and words. It was always traced that I was only temporary in his life. It hurt a lot. While my affection for him only grew stronger.

During my stay, I became friends with all the staff at the house, especially Grace Thompson.

As it turned out, Grace was a close friend of Alex's mother and had always looked after him when he was still a child. After Elizabeth's death, they lost touch for a while, but as soon as Frai got back on his feet and began to earn money, he searched for the woman and took her to live in his house. He wanted to provide her a quiet retirement, but this woman didn't know how to sit idle. So she declared herself a cook and took a place in the kitchen.

As soon as I had free time, I would run to Grace's kitchen and listen in awe to the various stories of Alex's childhood. We were often joined by the other workers in the house. Everyone listened, and no one believed that, once upon a time, Mr. Frai was a sweet, open, and sensitive boy. It was hard for everyone to imagine this always serious and busy man, as Grace described him in her stories. It surprised me a little because every time Alex and I were alone, he turned into a naughty boy, and we could laugh for hours on end. I wanted to believe that when he was with me, he could afford not to pretend and relax, that he trusted me that way.

Grace also told me about Elizabeth and the times they had worked together. From what she said, Alex's mom was a woman who was kind, beautiful, generous, and very naive. Grace said it was her naivety and her inability to stand up for herself that ruined her. I tried to find out exactly what happened to Elizabeth, but Thompson made it clear that she had no right to tell me. All I knew was that Alex's mother had suffered a tragedy that had left an indelible mark on his soul.

"Anna, you're here to see me?" Grace greeted me with a big smile. "I'm so glad you took the time to come. How are you doing?"

Grace Thompson had made me feel welcome the first time I met her. She was short, fit but not obese, with long, dark red hair. She also had amazingly kind brown eyes, a round face, and a wide smile. I absolutely loved spending time with her.

Today, she was teaching me how to make apple pie from Alex's mom's recipe.

"Everything's great. Nothing to complain about."

"And how are things with Sandro?" The woman asked and looked at me intently.

She used to call Alex Sandro and no other name. Before coming to Germany, according to his documents, he was Alessandro Moretti. But when he got his citizenship, he changed it to Alex Frai. The surname was not chosen by chance. In translation, it meant - "free". This way, he wanted to free himself from his father and have nothing to do with him.

"It seemed fine," I said and shrugged.

"It didn't sound very believable. Sweetie, you can tell me everything. You know everything stays within these walls and won't go anywhere else."

She sat me down at the table and looked intently into my eyes.

"In fact, everything is perfect. Alex is very sensitive, gentle, kind, and caring. Every day, it seems that I dissolve more and more in him."

"But?" The experienced woman immediately caught the catch.

"But... each time, he says it as if to remind me that the month has flown by and soon, five more will fly by like that, and that's where my time will be up."

"Can you elaborate a little bit more on the context of that?"

"That he was very wary of this period. He found it difficult to get along with someone, and in the end, a month has gone by like a day, and he's already looking forward to the other five going by just as quickly. When it's over, he'll get his prize, and I'll get mine."

"Where do you see the implication that it will be over between you two?"

"Yesterday, when we talked about it, he told me that he would fly to Italy, to this villa, and after that, he was planning a trip to America, for an unknown period of time and me..." tears came to my throat and with difficulty swallowing the lump, I continued, "I am not in his plans."

"Did you ask him if he wants to continue and what kind of relationship you have with him?"

"No, I'm scared. I haven't asked directly. It's just my guess, but if I ask, I might hear something that would break my heart."

"Well, if you live like that, you won't get very far. I know Sandro, and I see him glowing around you. I think even if he wanted to, he couldn't cut you out of his life so easily."

After some more talking, Grace calmed me down, and we started cooking. The recipe wasn't complicated. After quickly preparing it, I left to change and get the office ready for a regular client.

When I returned to my room, I found the flour was even in my hair. And since it was still an hour before the client came, I threw my clothes in the wash and decided to take a shower and let myself bask under the hot water jets.

Suddenly, I felt cold hands touching my stomach. I jumped and cried out in surprise.

"I'm sorry, I didn't mean to scare you," Alex said seriously.

"Why aren't you at work?" Trying to get away from the fright, I asked, diving into my roommate's arms.

"I just wanted to see you and surprise you."

He held me tightly against him, and I felt his heart pounding. There was something about his behavior that made me suspicious.

"Al, what's wrong?"

Releasing myself from his grip, I looked into my favorite blue eyes with anxiety in my heart.

"My men found Vicky today."

In his gaze, I could read anxiety, sadness, and fear. I'd never seen anything like it before.

"What's wrong with her?" I asked, barely audible, afraid of the answer.

"She's dead."

(Alex)

Someone declared war on me, and Vic's body was left outside the office. And judging by her thin body, she'd been held hostage for a long time.

As soon as I found out about it, I immediately left the place. On the way home, I was thinking only one thing — to get to Anna as soon as possible, to hug and feel her smell. All this time, I had convinced myself that she was just a temporary presence in my life. My feelings for her weren't real, and it all seemed like a game, but I just missed the moment when I started to dissolve into her. She had not only entered my house, but she had found her way into my heart, found my soul, and now she completely possessed it. The thought of someone could hurting my girl made my stomach churn.

At first, I didn't want to tell her the truth. I tried to shield her from all the bad things in the world. But knowing Anna's temper, she wouldn't just accept the new security system.

Now, standing in the shower with her and holding her tight, I'm glad she's okay.

"How? Why? And Jimmy, does he know yet?" Anna rushed questions in shock, pulling away and looking fearfully into my eyes.

"Shh, shh, shh. Come here."

I brought her back into my arms and tried to calm us both down.

"Jimmy knows and has volunteered to help Benjamin. They will investigate together."

"It's horrible. She was very young."

"Only six years older than you," I said and felt a lump in my throat.

"Why are you so scared? Do you think you're in danger?" Anna could see through me, no matter how hard I tried to hide my real emotions.

"I'm not scared for myself," I admitted honestly.

"Al, please tell me, are you in danger?" Anna cried and wrapped her arms around me tightly.

"I'm only afraid for you," I whispered, trying to hold on.

The emotions were so strong that I was overwhelmed.

I felt wild fear for her life, and I didn't realize how much I cherished this girl, my girl.

"Why? Does anyone need me?" She asked and rounded her already big eyes.

"I do. I need you like air. And if these people want to hurt me, they'll start with the most precious thing I have, and that's you. Once they have you, they'll have complete control over me."

Before I could finish the thought, a teary-eyed Anna threw herself on top of me, kissing me and wrapping her arms around my face.

For the first time, I didn't hide, not in front of her or myself, and told her how I felt.

"I want you," Anna whispered, looking into my eyes.

"Are you sure?"

"Yes."

I needed this intimacy as much as she did. I kissed her face, her neck, her shoulders, her heaving breasts. My hands caressed her entire body, stroking, squeezing, and pulling her to me. I was desperate to feel she was near and belonged only to me.

Picking Anna up in my arms, I carried her into the bedroom. Lowering her onto the bed, I looked into her eyes, savoring the desire that burned in her. It drove me as crazy as the curves of her body. In anticipation of intimacy, everything tantalized me and beckoned.

With my fingertips, I traced circles on her breasts, her belly, and her thighs. Each touch sent a wave of shivers through her and a thrill through me.

It seemed like an eternity since I'd waited to possess her. Kissing and nibbling her neck, I guided my hand to the inside of her thigh, slowly sliding upward. She moaned, entwined her hands in my hair, and began to arch toward my movements, giving me complete access to the most intimate parts of her body.

"I've waited so long for this. I want to savor you and every breath you take," I said.

Unable to contain myself, I lifted her by her hips, pulling her closer to me, spread her legs, and in one motion, I entered her sharply.

Tearing her moans from her lips, I penetrated her more deeply each time, finally feeling full power over her. The feeling was unparalleled. I gasped in the agony of passion, losing myself in her with each new movement.

Holding her hips, I thrust deep and hard into her womb like an animal off the chain, feeling the walls convulsively clench my penis, bringing me to ecstasy.

She was already screaming, her moans echoing around the room, and her arms wrapped around my neck, pressing her face against me.

"Don't close your eyes, look at me, feel inside you," I commanded, continuing to move inside her unceasingly until I felt her squeezing me inside with violent spasms.

I growled, made the final thrusts, and closed my eyes, giving myself over to the climax of the moment.

"Al, I love you," Anna whispered, panting.

"I love you, too."

I couldn't believe that I was capable of love. But I think that's what was happening to me.

"Promise to be careful and not to resist the security guards," I said seriously.

"I promise. But you promise to be there for me and not hide anything from me."

"I promise."

Chapter 24

"Where are you going in such a hurry?"

Alex didn't want to let me go and tried to hold me back by any means necessary, preventing me from getting dressed.

"I have a client coming in at four. I told you yesterday."

"How long is this going to take?"

"Two hours, and then I'm all yours," I murmured promisingly, kissed Alex, and hurried downstairs, putting on my sweater as I went.

I was happy to get back to work, as I was still shocked by the news. I couldn't believe that someone could just take a man's life like that.

My favorite client was already waiting for me in the lobby.

"Oh, hello. You look perfect today."

I greeted her with a genuine smile on my face.

She was dressed to the nines, as always. She wore a beige pantsuit, stiletto heels, and a bag from the latest collection of one of the top couturiers.

"Hey. I missed you so much. It feels like we haven't seen each other in forever. Come on, let's show me your new workspace."

I went downstairs and was just about to show the way to my office when Alex's voice came from behind me:

"What are you doing here? Did you find out about Vic yet?"

"Hey. Why are you home?" Stammering, asked my client and began to pale before my eyes.

"Alex, do you know Frau Masters?"

I also decided to put in my five cents and try to understand what was going on.

"Mrs. Masters is my sister," there was anger and irritation on Alex's face. "Lika, please explain what's going on."

"Alex, everything is not as it seems."

Mrs. Masters spoke confused and very nervous.

"No. Lika, no. You couldn't. I don't want to believe this," Alex was out of his mind. Abruptly turning to me, he grabbed my hand and, with maddened eyes, asked: "Did you know everything from the beginning? Was it all planned? How much did she pay you? Answer me!"

He shouted and looked at me with eyes that were not

his own. Everything inside me squeezed. I couldn't say a word out of shock.

"Let the girl go! Are you out of your mind? She didn't know anything. And you chose her yourself, or have you forgotten? The only thing I did was give her that green bracelet."

"And you don't think you did anything?! Just gave her the bracelet? You exactly knew I'd spot it. Like you exactly knew where she'd be. That's your whole plan? At what point was she supposed to leave — right before the finale, leaving me with nothing?"

"No, Alex, it's not like that. Cool down, please, and we'll talk."

But he wouldn't listen. He had a picture of his own version of reality in his head. And Frai just left, slamming the door loudly.

The ground went out from under my feet. I just sat on the floor, not realizing what my fault was.

How could he so easily assume that my feelings for him were just a game planned by someone else? The same thought kept spinning around in my head.

"Anna, I'm sorry. At least we can talk."

"Does that make sense?" I asked absentmindedly, at a complete loss.

"Look, I know him. He has a temper, but he needs time. Let's wash up, go out to the yard, get something to drink."

Lika helped me get up and walk to the guest bathroom. After I washed up, I calmed down a little and thought maybe she was right and I could explain to Alex that I had nothing to do with it. I didn't want to think of any other outcome.

We sat in the gazebo in the backyard. Nature was in full bloom. The days were warm, and summer was just a little while away. But I wasn't happy about it anymore.

"Alex had fallen head over heels in love with you. Klaus writes in every report about how my brother has changed since he's been with you," Lika said.

"Who's Klaus?"

"He's my men. He accompanies you everywhere you go. Haven't you noticed?"

"No. Alex always has guards with him, but I only know Jim since he's my driver and bodyguard, and Benjamin."

"Oh, there he is. Easy on the eyes. Klaus, come closer," Lika addressed someone behind me.

When I saw Klaus, I was almost dumbfounded. How could I not have noticed him before? He was an enormous man, shaven-headed, with the eyes of a serial killer and a large protruding jaw.

"In fact, I call it his superpower. At his size, he almost always goes unnoticed."

"Hello," I said in a slight stupor.

Stunned by the confusion of events, I felt empty inside.

"Good evening, Frau Anna," Klaus's voice was surprisingly soft and velvety. When he spoke, his whole demeanor softened at once.

"Klaus is German to the core. Herr Schmidt has been working for me for a very long time. Come, sit down with us."

Lika was very kind to the observer and looked at him warmly.

"In this house, he is your protection. Although, I know that Alex will never harm you. But I also know that sometimes he can bring you down with just a word."

Lika rolled her eyes at the last phrase.

"Frau Anna, if you want to leave the house and Alex prevents it in any way, you just need to go to any room with video surveillance and call me," Klaus said.

"Okay, thank you. But I have a strong feeling he'll kick me out as soon as he gets back," I replied sadly.

"Anna, give him time. He's entitled to a week's break, just like you. I have a feeling he's going to take it now," Lika said carefully.

My heart ached. Being without Alex all week and not

being able to talk to him seemed a terrible torture.

The most frustrating thing was that he'd made up his mind all at once and destroyed all the feelings we'd confessed just a few minutes ago.

"Angelica, why did you choose me?" I asked seriously.

"I'd been waiting for that question. The truth would have come out sooner or later, anyway. I wanted it to come out later than sooner," Angelica began bitterly, "Over the past year that we've known each other, I've realized that you and Alex have a lot in common. And it was hard not to notice how kind, sweet, and open-minded you are. That's exactly the girl I wanted to see around my brother. I know it doesn't sound right or even abnormal. But getting you two together in any other way was just impossible. You saw what he was like, practically a robot. And in the end, I was right. Alex seemed to come alive around you. He changed so much in just a month."

There was guilt in her voice for everything that had happened. At first, I felt angry at Lika, but after thinking for a second, I realized that she was right, and if it hadn't been for all of this, I would never have known the love I felt with Alex. However, right now, everything was in limbo.

"Why did you come here today?" I asked emotionlessly, feeling broken.

"I was pretty sure Alex wouldn't be home today. I know I shouldn't have taken that risk, but I really wanted to talk to you and see how you were."

"Why didn't Herr Schmidt tell you Alex was back if we were under his constant surveillance?"

It was strange to me that Herr Schmidt didn't warn Lika about Alex's presence in the house.

"After you and Alex had lunch, Klaus came to me with a report, and then we drove here together. My confidence in my brother's absence was reinforced by the fact that he had a crucial negotiation scheduled for this time. Alex had been working on this deal for three months already. And knowing him, he would never cancel this meeting."

I told Lika about the incident with Vic and why Alex had dropped everything and gone home. Horror showed in her big brown eyes. She knew Alex's secretary well and couldn't believe what had happened.

"Klaus, from now on, be close to Anna at all times, and not through the cameras," Lika told my new guard, he nodded in response and she turned to me. "I got you into this, and I won't forgive myself if something happens to you because of me."

I had more questions for Lika, but the news of Vic's death had scared her enough to make a few calls, and she hurried away, leaving me to Klaus.

Time seemed to slow down a lot since Alex had left. Sometimes it felt like time had stopped altogether.

With so many people in the house, I felt overwhelmingly lonely. Canceling all my clients, I spent entire days on the front porch, staring at the gate, hoping to see him.

During Alex's absence, I made friends with his dogs. Richard, Rick, and Rom were my best company. The three huge Dobermans ran up to me every time I went out on the porch and sat down beside me, resting their muzzles on my legs. They missed their master, too. We shared our sadness with the four of us.

On one such day, Julie arrived in another attempt to cheer me up.

"Why don't we go for a walk in the park?" She said with a hope in her voice.

"I'm sorry, but I don't feel like it."

"Anna, why don't we pick a new name for you, like Rose, and you can go live in the enclosure since you've been sitting here like a dog all day."

"Why not?"

I just shrugged. I didn't care where I was as long as I didn't have a foothold. This was getting really bad.

My friend tried to hug me, but the three dog faces

growled at the same time.

"Shh, it's okay," stroking, I calmed the dogs.

"Anna, I'm afraid of them."

"I used to be afraid of them too. They felt it, and we didn't get along at first. Try to see them not as a killing machine but as living creatures that need love and care."

But my friend just waved my words away and started looking for ways to cheer me up again.

"Hey, let's look at it this way. Frai ran away, but he sent an army to protect you, which means he cares about you. Isn't that right?"

"I'm not even sure how many of Alex's men are here and how many of Angelica's. And he could have given the order before he left, and now he doesn't give a damn about me. He's probably just protecting his house, not me. There's a lot of paperwork in here."

"Then check what exactly he's protecting," Julie said calmly.

"I promised him I'd be careful and stay under guard."

"Well, I seem to recall that he's broken his promises more than once."

There was truth in my friend's words. He had promised to be there for me...

Chapter 25

After thinking about Julie's words for a long time, I decided not to take any chances. I didn't know who the danger was coming from and what it could be fraught with in the aftermath.

I also didn't want to believe in the end of my and Alex's story. There was still hope in my heart that it would continue with a happy ending. There was a hole inside of me, eating away at me from the inside out, and it was getting bigger every day.

Every night, I dreamt of him calling me again, and I searched for him without success. In the previous month, the nightmares had all but stopped, but now I was even glad of them. At least this way, I could see his eyes.

On the sixth day of Mr. Frye's absence, I sat on the porch again, staring at the now-hated gate. Tailed friends sat beside me. In a moment, all three of them perked up, heads up and ears perked.

The gate opened, and a black, sporty Audi showed up. It was one of Fray's favorite cars. Silently, the car pulled up to the house, and I finally saw him.

Alex's face was impenetrable, like a mask. His eyes glassy, staring past me like I was an intangible ghost. He had a tired look, and his eyes testified to sleepless nights. His white shirt was crumpled, and his jacket was missing.

I wanted to jump up and hang around his neck, but fear stopped me — Alex looked dangerous. Even the dogs huddled against me. He passed by without a word.

At dinner, the game of silence continued. Alex was reluctant to put food in his mouth, picking at his plate and ignoring all my attempts to start a dialog. I noticed the wounds on his knuckles. They were bloody, but there was no answer to my question about what had happened.

Anger seized me, and I stood up from the table and headed to my room, packing my things. My body became active and energized as if I'd just woken up from a very long sleep. I wasn't to blame, but he'd decided to punish me. So now he was on his own.

While packing, I pulled out my phone and called my friend. I shared with her about everything that happened.

"So he just doesn't talk?" Julie asked.

"Yeah, he's completely ignoring my presence."

"Anna, maybe don't rush and give him some time."

"He had time. Do you have any idea what it's like to look at the person you love and see only ice in his eyes?"

"No, I don't, but you have to realize if you leave, it's over, completely and utterly. Are you ready for that?"

Tears came to my eyes, and I felt a lump in my throat. All the emotions I'd been holding back for days came rushing out.

"I don't want to, and I can't do it without him," I barely audibly squeezed out the words I was struggling to say.

"Then, gather all your remaining strength into a fist and prepare for battle."

"What do you suggest?"

"Memorize, or better yet, write it down..."

Mentally, once again, I thanked the universe for such a wonderful friend who was always ready to listen to me and support me. Although her advice was not always helpful, her ability to bring me to my senses was valuable.

After a while, just as I finished putting my things back together, Bennett knocked and asked me to join Mr. Frai. Wiping away my tears, I went with hope in my heart to the room where my impregnable fortress awaited me.

Alex was waiting for me in the home theater, and I sat next to him, but there was a barrier between us from the two armrests of our chairs. He'd chosen a documentary, as boring a movie as possible. For two hours I fought the urge to fall asleep with mixed success. He looked refreshed. But he seemed like he had not slept in ages. Leaning on his arm, pretty soon, Frai fell into slumber.

Julie suggested reaching out to him through intimacy, but the fear of being rejected was too strong. So I kept the distance he'd put between us. But I wasn't in any hurry to give up on the plan entirely.

The evening and night passed in silence. Alex lay down on his side of the bed and turned away from me. I wanted to hug him, to cuddle with my whole body, to smell his skin, to bury my hands in his hair, and to see his hazy gaze in return. Fighting myself and resisting the temptation, I turned my back the same way, trying to sleep.

Alex wasn't there when I woke up in the morning, but I could see the imprint of his massive hand on my stomach.

Perhaps, in an unconscious state, he couldn't resist and held me tightly in his sleep.

I pinned my hair into a high bun, threw off my clothes, and headed to the bathroom. I opened the door and gasped.

Frai was standing in front of me, in all his glory. He looked like a Greek god, droplets falling from his wet black hair and trickling down his neck to his collarbones, flowing over and connecting with the droplets on his torso, streaming lower and lower.

Biting my lip, I licked it dreamily, looking at the impressive size of the penis dangling between his powerful thighs.

Alex finished wiping himself off and threw the towel into the hamper, and I felt awkward, returning to reality. Coughing, I lowered my eyes to the floor and strode past him toward the shower, but I couldn't make it.

My tormentor turned around and grabbed me by the waist, pulling me to him, pressing my ass against his pubes, running one hand down my thigh, increasing the pressure, the other up to my chest, squeezing with the palm of his hand. The reaction followed lightning fast, shivers rippling through my body in waves. With his lips, he gripped my neck, nibbling gently. His breathing became heavy, and with my back, I could feel the frantic rhythm of his heart. Quite quickly, from my hip, his hand moved between my legs, fingering my most secret places.

"You're already ready," Alex mumbled with his low voice into the back of my head.

Abruptly, he lifted one of my legs giving himself access, and entered me in one motion, letting out a moan of pleasure. I gasped with desire, barely managing to clutch at the edge of the sink with my hands. His movements were sharp and hard. But they didn't hurt me, not even the opposite. Feeling the hot flesh inside me fill me completely, I moaned, moving against his thrusts and giving myself over to lust.

It wasn't like making love. It was more like quenching the thirst when you couldn't take it anymore. Increasing the tempo and thrusts, Alex penetrated deeper and deeper. Sweat rolled down our bodies, leaving wet traces, and his breath burned the back of my neck. After a couple of final thrusts, Frai pressed his wet forehead against my neck, breathing hard and shuddering.

Before I could gather myself, he was out of the bathroom, leaving me alone with resentment for such a brief and strange intimacy.

Chapter 26

At breakfast, Alex sat again with an impenetrable face and didn't even look in my direction. He pretended as if nothing had happened between us earlier in the bathroom.

Picking at my plate, I realized I couldn't eat a bite. I really wanted to run away, curl up on my pillow, and cry. But I continued to sit there, glancing at my watch and waiting for the end of this torture.

When the time was up, Frai threw the newspaper on the table and silently walked away.

I wanted to get up and leave, too. But instead, I continued to sit there as if I'd been nailed. I couldn't hold back my emotions any longer, and tears sprang from my eyes.

"My dear, what happened?" Grace's voice was gentle.

I didn't answer anything. I covered my face with my hands and continued crying. Grace hugged me tightly.

"Cry, my sweetheart, don't hold it in. I'm here, next to you. Everything will be fine," the woman said softly, stroking my head.

After crying enough, I started complaining about Frai like a little girl, pouring out my heart.

"He sees me as a piece of furniture he can use as he

pleases. I'm not a piece of furniture. I have feelings... He doesn't care about me," I sobbed, choking on a new wave of hysteria.

"Sweetheart, he does care. Believe me. He interrogated me last night about what was going on in his absence. He pretended to be interested in the general affairs of the house, but then he couldn't stand it and asked me directly about you."

I sniffled and stared at Grace, eagerly absorbing every word.

"Here, drink some water and eat something. You've gotten so skinny. The wind will soon blow you away."

She handed me a glass of water and moved the plate near to me. Her gaze was worried.

"And I told Alex he brought you to the end of your rope, that you didn't eat anything, and were on water alone. I also told him that when he was away, you sat on the porch immovable like a statue and waited for him to show up."

"What did he say?" I asked hopefully.

"I won't say anything else until you eat."

Grace moved my plate closer to me and paused, waiting. Without much enthusiasm, I had to put the food in my mouth, and then I stared at the woman in mute pleading.

"He didn't say anything, but I knew him. Sandro's nervous. He's wondering if he's doing the right thing. Give him some time. I know it's hard with him, but he doesn't know any other way."

"If he hasn't said anything, he doesn't care about me. He probably can't wait until the bet expires. So he can kick me out."

The bitter, hot tears kept streaming from my eyes.

"Do you remember those cufflinks with your initials that you gave Alex?" Grace asked excitedly.

Of course, I remembered them. Only a couple of weeks ago, Alex received them as my gift, put them on right away, and enjoyed them like a boy. But then he gave them to a jeweler for alterations. He asked him to inlay stones, green in one and blue in the other. He said it reminded him of my eyes and made cufflinks more particular.

"Yes, I remember," I replied, confused.

"Well, these cufflinks were on Sandro yesterday. That means they were ready when you two were already arguing. And he wore them anyway," Grace said with warmth.

That information didn't seem very relevant to me.

"It's not exactly a sign of affection, unlike his icy stares and that awful silence," I replied.

"Anna, do you really think this is the end?"

"I don't know. But I am more and more doubtful that I'm doing the right thing by staying here in this house."

"Then why don't you leave? I'm sure it's not because of the contract money."

"Because I love him. Even though I've been married, I've never felt anything like what I can feel now," I paused, holding back a flood of tears of self-pity, and added, "And if I leave, he won't get the villa. And that's crucial to him for some reason. How can I deprive him of it?"

"You can do anything, my girl. You have to decide what's most important to you. Put yourself at the top of your list and think about what's best for you," Grace said and stroked my hand.

"Thank you," I said quietly but sincerely.

I went to my room and just lay there staring at the ceiling until Bennett came in and told me that the car was waiting.

Slowly, I dressed and went to Frai's office.

At lunch, I had a sense of déjà vu, sitting on the couch in Mr. Frai's office with a lunchbox on my lap while he continued the meeting.

Leaning back on the couch, I fell into a long contemplation. Was there any point in fighting for him? Was I willing to put up with his heavy character? And what will be more difficult, to continue beating against the wall, hoping that he will change or try to forget him? And if I decide to fight and nothing happens, will I be able to survive the moment when he asks me to leave?

The most painful was the thought that if not for the terms of the bet, he would have gotten rid of me long ago.

The thought made me sad, and tears of self-pity sprang from my eyes. Covering my face with the palms of my hands, I stood up and wanted to escape without attracting attention, but my box fell with a clatter, and food flew in all directions. The noise drew the attention of everyone present, and all eyes turned to me. I blushed and ran out of the office.

On the way out of the building, I noticed Jimmy, who was having a very nervous conversation with Benjamin, the head of security.

"This can not be left like this. You must realize how it can turn out."

"Jim, you're being dramatic. Personal feelings are preventing your mind from seeing reality. Take a vacation and give yourself some time," said the head of security, giving a friendly pat on the guy's shoulder and heading for the exit.

I hadn't seen Jim since I'd heard about Vicki, and I hadn't had a chance to express my condolences to him. And Klaus was my new bodyguard, at Lika's insistence. Mr. Frai clearly didn't care about my safety under the circumstances.

"Hi, long time no see," I began awkwardly, "How are you?"

"Hello, Ms. Anna," Jim replied with a sad smile, "Are you okay?"

"Yes, as well as can be," I said with a strained smile.

My red, puffy eyes betrayed my condition, but I didn't want to draw attention to myself.

"Sorry to ask, but why weren't you at Vic's funeral? I understand you barely knew her, but it seemed you cared about her fate."

That question caught me off guard. I was so preoccupied with Alex. I didn't even think about Vicky's funeral.

"Jim, first, I'm so sorry. What happened to Vicky was horrible. She was a wonderful girl, and she certainly didn't deserve this. It's hard to imagine what you're going through right now. And please forgive my absence from the funeral. I wasn't aware of them."

"Thank you for your kind words. I'm glad you're not accusing her of every mortal sin."

"I'm sorry, but I don't really know what you mean. What is there to blame Vicky for?" I asked in surprise.

Jim looked at me incredulously.

"Mr. Frai didn't tell you anything?"

"No. And I'd really appreciate it if you'd tell me."

As the story unfolded, I became increasingly uneasy. It was hard, almost impossible, to believe what I was hearing.

According to Jimmy, Alex and his team, together with the police, had been investigating the case for the last six days. The evidence they found indicated that Vicky was a mole in Frai's company. When she lost her job, she was kidnapped and held for a while in hopes of somehow still using the girl. But as soon as they realized that she was of no use to them, they killed her and dumped her body near the main office.

Alex and his team even managed to find out who was a customer of this murder. That was one of the victims of the anti-advertising company. But they couldn't catch him yet, as he disappeared from the country without a trace.

"But I don't believe it. Vic couldn't have leaked the information. She had a good salary, and her family are pretty well-off people. And I don't see any motive why she would do that," Jim summarized, "I've collected all the copies of the paperwork on this case, and I want to check it all over again. I just can't leave everything like that."

Out of the corner of my eye, I saw Klaus talking on the

phone to someone and squinting in our direction. Apparently, Frai or his sister didn't want to let me in on the details and probably instructed him to make sure I didn't find out anything.

But there was something about the whole story that didn't add up. And since I didn't care about Alex's instructions, I shamelessly suggested that Jim run away and check it together.

To my surprise, he was enthusiastic about the idea. And pretty quickly he was able to come up with an escape plan.

"Tell him you need to use the ladies' room. There is one on the first floor just down the hall and a window there. I'll be waiting for you on the other side. And it's best if you leave your cell phone and your shoes. There's a tracking chip in there. They'll find us right away. And I think they won't pat our heads."

After a little thinking, the guy asked if I was sure of my decision.

"Yes," I answered firmly.

Chapter 27

Finding out that I had chips on me made my decision many times more sure. Inside me, everything was boiling with anger. Alex thought he could keep me on a short leash, but he was wrong.

Parting ways with Jim in a meaningful manner to lull the vigilance of my bodyguard, I headed towards the girl at the reception and inquired about the location of the restroom. I asked Klaus to wait for me at the exit of the building.

Before I left my phone on the sink, I quickly typed a text for Julia, "I don't know what I'm signing up for, but I'm fine. Cover me if possible, and don't worry."

I took off my shoes, took a deep breath, and proceeded as planned.

The window opened without difficulty. On the other side, the former driver was already waiting for me and helped me out. As soon as I stepped barefoot on the still cold ground, I shivered from the cold.

"We must take public transportation. My car has a tracker, too," Jim told me.

"There's a chance I won't be able to get very far barefoot," I said through gritted teeth.

"Here, put on my shoes. There's a store around the corner, and I'll buy you something. But we have to move fast. According to the regulations, the guard will go to check on you in fifteen minutes. If he doesn't get an answer within five minutes, the door will be opened. It'll take another ten minutes for the universal key card to be brought in. And then we only have half an hour to spare."

Jim explained all the details to me as he went along, not faltering, not even out of breath. Only now, I noticed the perfect training of the guy. Against the background of the other guys from the guards, he always seemed to be the weakest and not particularly noteworthy.

We turned the corner and found ourselves in front of a small shoe store. Grabbing the first pair of shoes from the showcase, my escape partner quickly paid for the goods in cash, and we set off towards the subway.

As I settled into the seat, I took a breath, knocked down by the rapid stride, and, after catching my breath, decided to find out what we would do next.

"Where are we going?" I asked.

"Since they pinned everything on Vick, I rented an apartment and started collecting copies of all the paperwork and evidence, but nothing helpful was found there. I'm a security guard. I know how to rescue and protect, but I have no idea how to find a lead."

"Can Alex find this apartment?" I inquired.

"With his connections, he can find anyone, but it'll take time. I'm guessing about 24 hours."

"Then we have time. Can I ask you a couple of off-topic questions?"

"Yeah, sure."

"When were chips put in my shoes? And why the shoes?" I was still shocked after knowing of its presence.

"Your phone has a native tracker. They just installed the program right after you signed the contract. And they put chips in your shoes the day after they found out about Vic. That was in case you were kidnapped. Statistically, kidnappers don't leave victims barefoot."

"I'm glad they didn't integrate anything into me," I pointed.

"Well..." Jim's extended "well" made me jump up and start groping myself. "You're not wearing anything. Please sit down. We'd better not attract attention."

The former driver laughed at me.

"Who knows what Alex might have been up to?"

"In fact, Mr. Frai had considered it, but in the end, he hadn't made up his mind."

That information made my throat lumpy.

"Except I don't think he cared very much. He was just

afraid that if I was kidnapped, he'd lose the bet," I said quietly.

"Mr. Frai is a pretty private person and didn't share his experiences with me, but I don't think he was thinking about the bet at that moment. He's been watching you on the cameras. He's been distracted. He hasn't eaten much, and he hasn't slept much," the guy said.

I realized that he was worried, too. Alex let me into his world, and opened up to me, which was extremely difficult for him, and after the situation with Lika, he was just scared. That's why he ran away, trying to avoid more pain.

"And one more question — why are his hands knocked down in blood?" I asked guiltily, understanding Jim had brought me along not for this interrogation.

"He overheard you talking to your friend on the veranda. When Julie suggested you check out what he really cared about, his emotions got the best of him. So Mr. Frai decided to let them out on the punching bag, no gloves. I think he was afraid you'd do something stupid," the guy replied and grinned crookedly.

"Thank you Jimmy," I said, immersed myself in my thoughts.

It took us over an hour to get to our destination, with several transfers. At one point, I realized I didn't know where I was. We were already far outside the city.

The apartment itself was in a high-rise building in an unsightly neighborhood. I felt uncomfortable with the surroundings. An empty street, high fences, broken windows in the houses, and graffiti all over the walls.

"Not a very welcoming neighborhood. Maybe we should have tried to bring all the documents to Alex's mansion and go through them there," I suggested.

"Mr. Frai closed the case. It's all very convenient, and no one wants to bother. And if they didn't tell you anything, I don't think they'd let us do it in peace."

"But they never found the customer of murder. Why did they close the case then?" I wondered.

"Surveillance has been set up behind the client's house and all his acquaintances, and he didn't seem particularly dangerous to Mr. Frai," Jimmy answered, shrugging his shoulders.

This story was getting stranger and stranger to me.

We went into one of the buildings and went up to an apartment much appropriate for this area, with white walls and peeling paint, windows with broken blinds, and a worn floor with strange stains. The whole place was one room and a bathroom, which I didn't even want to look into. The only furniture was a kitchen set with sagging doors and a mattress on the floor with many boxes of documents around it. This environment made the feeling of discomfort many times greater.

"Are these the documents?" I asked.

"Yes, absolutely all copies. I'm sure I haven't missed a single piece of paper," Jim reported proudly.

"Then I'll go through them," I said.

"Do you mind if I get some coffee?"

"Yeah, sure."

"Can I get you some?" Jim offered.

"I'd like some. Thank you."

Luckily, I had a blanket thrown over the mattress, clean enough on first inspection. I settled down on it and began to sort through the papers.

There was a lot of stuff in that pile of papers — all the calls made from Alex's waiting room, the information on Marcus Fisher, who seemed to be just the kind of client who wanted revenge. And all the information on Vic.

I wanted to do as much research as I could. The more I delved into the case, the more questions I had. But I couldn't formulate an exact thought. Something obvious was eluding me.

Jimmy had long since returned with the drinks and watched me intently without making a sound.

Chapter 28

I spread out all the paperwork, checking the numbers of incoming and outgoing calls, separately spread out the map I'd made of the radio towers, and tried to piece together a coherent picture.

My dad was a retired investigator, and I often had to go to his office, listen to how they worked cases, and looked for clues. I tried to work along the same lines, hoping I'd picked up some of his deduction.

"So, I have a question and maybe a theory," I said, standing up but not taking my eyes off the papers, "We are starting from the version that Vic was not a mole. But it's clear that someone still leaked the information because we know that the client base was copied. So her killer is the real rat. So Marcus may not be the real mastermind behind this, but just another set-up to throw us off. There's a map right here of where he made the calls to the front desk. What if we check the cameras in the area and see if Marcus was even there? If he wasn't there, that would be a reason to reopen the case."

"That's a good idea," the guy said thoughtfully, and after doing some calculations in his head, he added, "No one checked that, but I'm afraid the search area would be too big, and I don't think it would be possible to track anyone down."

"And we're running out of time. They probably don't keep camera footage for long. But if we can prove Marcus is not involved, it'll at least launch a new investigation. I don't think it'll exonerate Vic, though. All the paperwork points to her. And if I understand correctly, she was the only one who had access. Which means my theory doesn't make sense."

"Alex is very caring about protecting information. Vicky was the only one who knew about the database."

"How close were you to her?" As if, by the way, I

asked.

"You don't suspect me, do you?"

Jim's face instantly changed, and a strange grin appeared on it. Even though I was absorbed in the task at hand, I watched his reaction closely as I voiced my final thoughts. He was clearly nervous and even called Alex by his first name instead of the obligatory "Mr. Frai."

Since I'd gone with the theory that Alex's secretary had nothing to do with it, it looked like Jimmy might still have access since he'd been hanging around Vic the whole time.

"Suspecting you would be stupid. Why would you bring me here? If you're the killer, the case is closed. Why would you want to reopen it?" I asked with a nervous chuckle and felt a chill run down my spine.

"Well, maybe to kill you, as it is an order from the real customer. And at the same time, to check again the documents for the presence of tails behind me," the guy answered absolutely calmly, keeping a grin on his face.

His words made the papers slip from my grasp, and a veil of darkness started descending before my eyes.

"We're in no hurry? Can I at least know everything before I die?" I asked with a trembling voice, hoping to delay the inevitable and try to find a way to escape.

"We're in no hurry. You're doing a great job. You followed all the instructions and won us the time. And you know, in a way, I've grown attached to you, much like I did with Vick. Killing her was harder than I thought. It's going to be easier with you, of course. But don't get me wrong, my conscience will haunt me for a couple of days," my executioner said without a shadow of sincerity. "So what exactly do you want to know?"

"Who is the true customer, and why would he want me dead?" I asked and felt that my fingertips were numb with fear.

"Christopher Davis, but that name doesn't mean anything to you. He's a wealthy and powerful man. Frai's company did a lot of damage to his reputation a couple of years ago. And later, on Davis' orders, I joined Alex's service. Revenge was going to be big, but without bloodshed: total collapse of the company, exposure with all the consequences, and so on. But Frai, to top it all off, slept with his daughter. Naturally, Christopher couldn't stand it, so he decided to sting harder — kill you and then bring down the company."

"When did he sleep with her?" suddenly, it just came out of my mouth.

I was surprised by my question. But based on the situation, Alex's contact with the other girl wasn't a while ago.

Did he sleep with her when we were already together? I thought to myself.

"Oh, how sweet is that. You're about to die, but you think about the loyalty of that emotionless heartbreaker. Although to be fair, you did manage to melt his heart. It was fun to watch him suffer when he thought you could be attacked," Jim looked at me with pity. "He slept with her before he met you. So you can relax. In that idiotic bet, she was the first girl Lika happened to choose. Can you imagine such a coincidence?"

For a moment, I was relieved, but soon, I remembered that I was on death's doorstep, and panic set in again.

"Why do you hate him so much? You obviously have some personal grudge against Alex."

"Why love him? I had a perfect track record. But when I got my assignment and joined his service, I was only an errand boy for the first year. Later, I was promoted to driver and chaperone for the escort girls. Do you realize how humiliating that is? And to top it off, I was assigned to you to fulfill your needs. But my relationship with Alex is irrelevant. He's just my job."

"What are you going to do after you kill me? Won't they find out?" I kept asking questions, hoping to buy more time.

"No. By the street cameras they won't be able to track

our location until tomorrow morning. That gives me enough time to make it look like I'm going to get rid of all suspicion," Jim said calmly and a little bored.

"How?"

"Marcus is being held hostage on the floor above. I'll kill you first, then him, and of course, I'll hurt myself. I'll make it look like we were working on a case, and we were attacked. I'll get fired, of course, but I've already got all the data I need. So, all I have to do is wait for the right moment and pass it on."

"Why did you kill Vic?" I kept stalling and frantically thinking about how to escape.

"Quite a lot of questions, don't you think? I'm getting kind of tired of talking. And you know, I got a lot of work to do."

"This is the last one, I promise," I said, almost in a whisper, realizing that death was approaching and that there was no chance of escape.

"Okay, you've got me, but only because you are a good person. Anyway, I liked Vic a lot, and sex with her was just fire. But she had one significant disadvantage: she was super curious. She always knew everything about everybody. At some point, she began to follow me and even realized I was copying the base, but she couldn't prove it. I had to set her up. So Alex would fire her and forget about her. I held her hostage for my own pleasure, but then I got the order to kill you, and the plan took definite shape."

Jim said scary things in a completely casual tone.

Then he straightened up and took a pistol and a silencer out of his jacket pocket. Fear gripped my whole body, and the tension at the back of my head felt like a thousand needles.

"Will it hurt me?" I asked in a weak voice and felt my heart beating so hard it felt like one more beat, and it would burst out of my chest.

"You said the last question," Jim said with a sneer, but

then calmly added, "No, I'll make it quick. I promise."

He stood next to an old kitchen set, pulled a portable speaker out of a drawer, and turned on some music, turning the volume to full blast. After that, my executioner started screwing the silencer onto the muzzle of the gun, doing it slowly and concentrating. It seemed to me that it gave him a lot of pleasure. Deciding to seize the moment, I desperately rushed towards the door, but he immediately intercepted me and forcefully pushed me away. Falling to the floor, I painfully hit my head, and the rest unfolded quickly, just as Jim had promised.

I didn't have the courage to watch the trigger pull. I covered my face with my hands and tensed my body.

The last thing I heard was a deafening gunshot that, despite the loud bass, broke from the melody's rhythm. A sharp pain shot through me and took over my entire body. The pain was so intense that I couldn't even open my eyes or cry out. It completely paralyzed me. After a moment, I felt the darkness begin to envelop my consciousness and draw me away. I didn't resist and obediently followed it.

Chapter 29

Somewhere very far away, voices and scraps of phrases came to me.

"Did you do all that was possible? Then do the impossible!"

"Please calm down..."

And darkness again. No thoughts or images. Nothing but emptiness and stillness.

"You need to get some sleep. You can hardly stand on your feet anymore."

"Go away, leave me alone! The only thing I need is for her to wake up."

"Anna's a fighter. She'll wake up, and it would be nice for you not to go completely insane by then."

"Go away! Just go away!"

The voices were distinct this time and seemed familiar. I wanted to join the conversation, but the darkness once again carried me far away from here, plunging me into complete peace.

"Lika, did you hear that?" A familiar voice broke into a scream full of pain and despair, "Did you hear what he said? There's nothing more they can do!"

"Alex, let the doctor go! Look at me. You're out of control."

"I can't take it anymore. Wake her up. You always know everything. Bring back my Anna, I beg you, please..."

A man's voice screamed, cried, and begged. Every word he spoke echoed inside me with a strange feeling. All the calm that the darkness had given me evaporated in an instant. I couldn't bear to stay in it any longer.

I tried to move, or at least twitch, to signal that I could hear. Through my tightly clenched eyelids, I felt a faint light, followed by a discomfort in my throat and an unbearable pain in my shoulder.

"Anna?! Can you hear me? Call a doctor! Now!" A man's voice shouted somewhere near me.

The room abruptly filled with noise. There was a mass of people around me. Someone was saying something, and I could feel them tugging, turning, and manipulating me. But the pain overshadowed everything, seeping into every cell and filling my body with unbearable agony.

The darkness began to creep up again, and I wanted to follow it so that everything would end. I wished to stop what was happening because I couldn't take it anymore.

"I love you! Don't go! Don't leave me! Anna, please!"

That voice drowned out all the noise in the room. It made me chase away the tantalizing darkness and fully accept the pain.

Continuing to struggle, I managed to open my eyes. The light hit them painfully, and I immediately clenched my eyes shut, but a few tries later, I managed to get used to it.

Doctors and nurses were running around me, saying and asking me something, but I just blinked back. I couldn't speak yet.

"Now they will give you a painkiller, which will make you sleep," the doctor said.

I shook my head negatively.

"It's okay, don't panic. Your body needs to recover. The main thing is that you regained consciousness. Everything bad is behind. Now, only recovery and..."

I didn't get to hear the rest of what the doctor told me. My sleep took me far away from what was happening.

In the dream, I was walking through a familiar maze. And it was no longer a nightmare. The sun was shining brightly, illuminating my path. The hedges were strewn with red roses, nothing clung to my clothes, and walking was easy. As I turned the corner, I saw the exit. The intense glow blinded me, but with no fear, I stepped confidently into the unknown and found myself in a green clearing. I stepped barefoot on the soft grass that tickled my feet so affectionately. As I walked forward, I saw a large tree. A man was lying under it and admiring the sky. I hurried to get closer and saw that the man was Alex. His beautiful face was flooded with warm light, and he wore a white, loose shirt and pants. I noticed that I was also wearing a white, airy dress, decorated with a scattering of beads. With a sweet smile, Alex reached up, took my hand, and drew me to him. Our lips intertwined in a tender kiss. A feeling of happiness filled me.

"I finally found you. You have no idea how long I've been looking for you," my voice echoed through the clearing.

"You've found something more — my soul. It belongs to you now."

"How can that be?" I asked, staring into his eyes.

"Why not? Don't you feel that we are connected now?"

"I feel so happy to be here with you. I don't need anything else."

"We'll always be together now, no matter what happens. But now you have to come back. The people who care about you are waiting for you. That includes me," he smiled broadly and kissed my temple, pulling me tight against him.

I didn't want to wake up, but my eyes were foggy, and I felt like I was falling.

I tried to open my eyes, and this time it was easier.

"Al, look!" I heard a familiar female voice.

"Hey," whispered the man who had brought me back to life.

Through the veil before my eyes, I saw Alex and Lika in front of me. An exhausted Frai held my hand tightly and kissed every finger on it. Angelica stood behind him, tears streaming down her face.

"You don't look so good," I said in a hoarse, weak voice.

"Why did you scare me so much?" Alex moved closer to me and pressed his forehead against mine.

"You shouldn't have ignored me," I joked, though it was hard to speak.

"Guilty as charged. I hope you can forgive me," Frai whispered in his softest voice and rubbed his nose against my cheek.

"I don't think I have any other choice," I said with a smile.

"Anna, I'm an idiot and the dumbest person on this planet. I'm sorry for what I did. If you say you don't want to see me anymore, I'll understand."

Alex had tears in his eyes. He sounded completely sincere.

"Let's put this behind us, shall we? I love you," I said and felt myself tear up, too.

"Anna, you're everything to me," Alex whispered.

Our idyll was broken by the doctor, who came to examine me and pleased me with the news about the upcoming long recovery. Then he wrote out his prescriptions and left.

As it turned out, Jim's bullet had hit me in the shoulder, miraculously not shattering the joint but hitting some vein. The painful shock of the bullet knocked me unconscious. Despite the fast arrival of the ambulance, a coma occurred because of the loss of blood.

After the doctor left, Lika kissed me on the cheek, wished me a speedy recovery, and went home to rest, still with tears in her eyes.

Alex and I were left alone in the room. I tried to send him home to sleep and recover, but he was adamant.

"Am I boring you that much?" Alex asked.

With a satisfied smile, my man stretched out on the bunk beside me, on my left side, where no IV tubes were sticking out of my arm.

"Is that possible? I feel like I haven't seen you in forever. By the way, how long was I unconscious?"

A grimace of pain appeared on Alex's face after my question, and he rubbed his eyes, chasing away the coming tears.

"Two weeks, but it felt like a lifetime," Frai clung to me like he was afraid I was going to disappear, "Every day, I felt like a part of me was dying. The doctors made no prognosis, gave no hope, and just told me to wait."

"But it's okay now, I'm with you," I squeezed his hand tightly to confirm my words, "Al, you really should get some sleep. You're exhausted."

It seemed that looking into his beloved and dear face, I

saw another person, sharply aged ten years. There were gray hairs in his pitch-black hair, and red capillaries surrounded the iris of his eye, which was as blue as a clear sky. His eyelids were swollen, and deep bags were visible beneath them.

"Can I stay?" Alex asked, yawning and settling on my healthy shoulder, and fell asleep almost immediately without waiting for an answer.

Chapter 30

I had many questions, but the one who could answer them was sleeping soundly next to me.

Luckily for me, Julie came into the room soon enough. She didn't look so good either, pale as a wall and with expressive bruises under her eyes.

"Anna, you... I'm going to kill you!"

With wet eyes, my friend ran up, gently pressed herself against me, and kissed me on the forehead.

"Get in line because there are too many people who want it. And don't make any noise, you see, the man is sleeping," I hissed.

"I don't think anything will wake him up now. He's completely malnourished. They even put him on IVs because it was impossible to get him to eat. Grace was the only one who could get the stubborn one to eat sometimes," she lamented, settling into the chair next to the bed.

"Julie, I'm so sorry. I don't know what I was thinking," I squeezed my friend's hand tightly and asked, "How are my parents? Do they know?"

"Yes. And Alex arranged for them to come here. Now, they are in the mansion. We all took turns guarding you, including Lika. Except no one replaced your prince. He was rooted to the spot and it was impossible to move him.

By the way your parents will be here soon," after a little silence, she added, "You scared us all to death. Promise not to do that again."

"Never again, honestly."

"How are you feeling?" Julie asked worriedly.

"I've been better, but I'll live. Of course, if you believe the doctor's assurances," I tried to joke, and my friend just grinned wryly, "Jules, do you know how I was found? What happened? I remember only the sound of the gunshot and then a blackout."

"Your rose quartz pendant helped in the search."

"What? It's got a tracker on it, too?" I was surprised.

"Yes. Alex suspected someone in the entourage might be untrustworthy and he secretly set up additional tracking."

"But I never took off the pendant. How did he do it?" I asked in surprise.

"You'll have to ask him because I don't know," Julie said, waving her hands.

I'll have to talk with Alex seriously about his obsession with following me. But I'll do it later. Now, he's unlikely to hear or understand what I want him to understand. I made a note for the future in my mind.

With a lump in my throat, I asked Julie what I was most concerned about.

"Why," I paused and took a deep breath, "Why did Jim miss?"

My question made my friend shiver.

"I think I'll start at the beginning. The beacon in your pendant wasn't stable, and it took quite a while to get an accurate location. Apparently, because you had a long subway ride, the signal from the tracker was often lost. And the most difficult thing was to find the proper apartment. People were divided into groups. One group would go and break down the doors, going up the floors. The other group went down the ropes, looking through the windows. At some point, both groups were attracted by loud music, and everyone rushed over there. The first one on the right floor was Beni," Julie struggled to say the words, but she continued, "When he saw you, he broke the window and flew in, pushing Jim just as the shot was fired, causing him to miss."

"Oh, wow. But who's Beni?" I wondered.

"Benjamin Steele, Alex's head of security," she blushed.

"When did he become Beni?" I looked at her meaningfully.

"He was on duty in the corridor and brought me food. We often had coffee. And, somehow, he became Beni, but that's another story. And by the way, I found out everything from him," she justified herself, blushing again.

"Now it's clear. While I was fighting for life, you were fighting for love," I teased.

"You're such an asshole."

We laughed, which made the peacefully sleeping man fidget in my arms.

"Where was Alex?" It was the second question, which worried me just as much.

When Julie heard it, her face changed again, and her voice started trembling.

"In the other group, they had by then also climbed to the proper floor, but they didn't know which door was the right one. Then a gunshot rang out, and Frai rushed to the sound, knocking the door off its hinges with a single blow. When he entered the room, he saw you in a pool of blood on the floor. Beni said he'd never heard people scream like that. Everyone in the room was stunned and couldn't even move. Alex clamped down on the wound, trying to stop the blood, but there was too much of it."

Tears rolled down Julie's cheeks.

"Hey, it's over," I wanted to calm down my friend, but it was like she didn't hear me, mentally traveling back in time.

"I still remember the moment when I saw him when I arrived at the hospital..." she sighed heavily, "You were being operated on, and he was standing in the middle of the corridor, covered in your blood. He was thrashing around like a wounded animal, screaming, falling on the floor, hitting the wall with his hands. Everyone was afraid to go near him. Only Lika dared. She clasped him in her arms and wouldn't let go. We were all scared for you, but his pain had no comparison."

Hot tears ran down my cheeks. Alex had already suffered the loss of his mom, and in doing so, he'd lost a part of himself. For a long time, he'd been hiding behind his endless work and not allowing himself to live life to the fullest. With my appearance in his life, Alex decided to take a risk and opened up, allowing himself feelings and emotions. And once again, he was on the verge of losing someone he loved. My heart snapped at the realization of the pain he'd endured these days. Turning my head, I greedily pressed my lips to his stubbly cheek.

"Anna, are you all right?" Alex asked, waking up instantly and looking at my crying face with sleepy eyes.

"I love you, and I'm really sorry."

"Shh, it's okay," Frai said with a sigh of relief and added with a smile, "And don't worry. As soon as you get better, I'll deal with you for your recklessness and running away."

His lips found mine, and it was the most tender and promising kiss.

Chapter 31

After a week, I was finally able to move around unaided. Of course, I did not run like a young gazelle yet. But I was able to win the race to the candy machine of my neighbor from the ward across the hall. He was already at a very respectable age and could only get around with a walker, but you can't judge the winners.

My parents and Julie stayed in my room, and we talked and played board games for days.

The first time I met my parents, they gave me a hug but then went on to lecture me for hours about "how I could do this to them." They had a whole list of complaints, and unfortunately, everything was to the point, so I just listened, nodded guiltily, and vowed to be cautious and careful.

Alex ran in for a while but then disappeared at work. Considering all the events, he had a lot of things to do.

The whole floor was covered with security guards, and all the doctors and nurses were being scrutinized. Each of them did not forget to blame me and remind me that I was in the hospital. And how it was preventing them from doing their job. In response, I just shrugged my shoulders, as I had no opportunity to influence what was happening.

After a while, I was discharged from the hospital for home medical care. I was happy. Although the ward was non-standard and had all the amenities but it was still a bit dreary. But at home, the walls heal, and, in addition, there is a double bed.

At the mansion, I was greeted with a kind welcome. Grace had prepared an unbelievable amount of goodies. Bennett wore a tailcoat. The only thing missing was the red carpet and Alex, who was at work. Apparently, the only way I could keep him around was if I was dying.

Over the next two weeks I worked hard on my recovery. A trainer with a medical background and obvious talent helped me a lot. He managed to get me in pretty good condition in a short period of time.

The only frustrating thing was the regular absence of my beloved man by my side.

In order not to repeat the mistakes of the past, without looking for workarounds, I waited for his return late at night and decided to talk.

When Alex came quietly into the bedroom, I turned on the light sharply, letting him know he couldn't fall asleep quickly.

"Am I in trouble?" My man asked anxiously.

"You guessed it. I love your insight," I said affectionately.

"What did I do wrong?" Frai asked, throwing off his jacket and sitting on the bed.

"You're distancing yourself from me again. You don't say anything about what's going on, and you disappear all day long."

"I'm sorry, there's been too much going on. I just need a little more time to get things straightened out. And I promise to spend a lot more time with you when I figure things out," Alex said and turned his back to me and started to undress.

"Don't you want me anymore?" I barely heard myself ask.

It was the question that pained me the most. The last time we'd been intimate had been before the attack, and it was hardly intimacy. And since I'd been released from the hospital, Alex hadn't even tried to make a vulgar innuendo.

Alex turned sharply to me and rounded his eyes.

"This is where the doctor gets all the blame. He made it clear that you need to recover," he said with a hurt tone.

"Al, I've been going for a run every morning. And today, I was able to run four kilometers. It's been almost a month and...

I couldn't finish the sentence. Alex kissed my lips greedily, invading my mouth with his tongue, caressing it passionately and tenderly at the same time. A pleasant shiver ran through my body, and my lower abdomen ached in anticipation of the continuation.

I buried my hands in the hair of the object of my passion, not letting him pull away from me and not wanting to break the kiss. My whole body shivered with desire.

"Stop, we have to be careful," Alex whispered into my face, pulling his lips away from mine.

"I need you. I don't want to be careful. I want you," I replied, panting, pulling him into the kiss again.

I used my left hand to undo the buttons on his shirt, exposing his manly chest. Then I ran my fingertips over his skin, barely touching and teasing my partner. He sucked in air noisily, lifting and hovering over me. Alex's eyes darkened with desire, and my insides clenched at the sight of him.

My man tore off his shirt in one fell swoop, followed by his white undershirt, revealing a flawless torso.

I wanted to touch him with my hand and run it over the oblique muscles of his abdomen, but, with a cocky grin, Alex deflected, not letting me reach him.

"Hey, what are you doing?" I was outraged.

"I made a promise to you at the hospital, and I intend to keep it," Alex said in a low profound voice.

His eyes flickered. I felt a lump in my throat and started fidgeting under him.

"Take off all your clothes. I don't want to hurt you. Your arm still hasn't fully recovered," Frai ordered, climbing off me.

I stood up obediently, looked him in the eye, and slowly pulled down the straps of my silk nightgown, letting it slip off my body and fall to my feet, revealing my naked body to him. I prudently left my underwear off.

The reaction from him was immediate. He came over and put his hand on the back of my head, weaving his fingers into my hair, tilting my head back, and pressing his forehead against mine.

"You're driving me crazy, and I accept it. I won't resist my feelings anymore. I want to savor every day with you," Alex whispered against my lips.

He pushed me against the wall and put my leg over his thigh. He stood back a little, admiring my body, and ran his fingers along the curves, caressing my skin. Looking me in the eye, Alex moved his hand from my stomach down to the most sensitive area, massaging and pressing.

He watched my reactions intently.

Alex stopped every attempt I made to touch him. Deftly intercepting my hands, he continued to tease me. Got me almost to the edge, he stopped, removing his hand and switching to caressing my breasts, and then Alex started all over again. My head was spinning, and my lungs were short of air.

"I will torture you with caresses," my man whispered hoarsely into my ear.

Unable to stand, I pushed Frai away and slid down the wall to my knees.

Alex got nervous and wanted to lean toward me, but I managed to grab the belt on his pants and unbuckle it. He hadn't expected that. Taking him by surprise, I bought time and quickly released his erect penis from his pants. With my lips around the flesh, I began to caress the tip with my tongue. Alex immediately responded with a moan of pleasure, thrusting his hips forward and penetrating deeper into my mouth.

I took him completely, swallowing, moistening, caressing, and nibbling. I built up the pace and thrust in and out, teasing, playing with his lust. I reveled in his pleasure and fueled my desire even more. When he was almost at his limit, Alex freed himself, picked me up, and sat on the edge of the bed, placing me on top of him. He penetrated me slowly, letting me feel every inch of him, feeling him gradually fill me.

Our moans intertwined. We were both burning with passion and lust. Alex lifted his hips, and I pressed myself against his body, allowing him to enter as deeply as possible. We adjusted to each other's rhythm, speeding up and slowing down, letting the moment take us over completely. It was a total merger between us.

My hands rested on his shoulders and fingernails left red marks on his soft skin. His hands gripped me tightly, sliding from my waist to my hips, up to my breasts, caressing my protruding nipples and giving me intense pleasure.

When I felt his muscles stiffen, his whole body tense and trembling, I followed him. My lips against his cheek, panting, I savored the orgasm that overtook us, so vivid and passionate.

Tired and sweaty, we collapsed on the bed.

"Anna, you surprised me again," Alex said, trying to catch his breath.

"I hope it was pleasant," I murmured, settling down on his broad chest.

"Exactly."

Sleep came over us in each other's arms.

Chapter 32

In the morning, to my delight, Alex was still beside me. He was sleeping quietly, snuggled against my neck and holding me close. As I admired him, I gently ran my hand along his shoulder, up to his neck, and placed my palm on his cheek, stroking it with my thumb.

"Good morning," Frai whispered in a smile, not opening his eyes.

"Good morning. It's so pleasant to wake up next to you."

"It won't be long before it's like this every morning. Trust me."

"I trust. I always trusted."

He opened his eyes, rubbed the tip of his nose against my cheek, and pulled me closer.

"You know what would make this morning even better?" Alex asked conspiratorially, moving his hot palm to my chest.

"Why don't you tell me, or better yet, show me?" I asked in a whisper, arching my back and sticking out my bare chest.

"I will, and I'll do it with great pleasure," the tempter's voice was low and hoarse.

Alex turned me back to him and pressed my ass against his pubes, where I immediately felt the hard flesh pressing against me. His hand squeezed my thigh and slid down between my legs. Running his fingers over the most sensitive areas, he sharply penetrated me with one of them. I didn't linger and let out a moan of pleasure.

"You're always ready for me so quickly," Alex whispered softly, biting my earlobe.

I only moaned again as his deft hands caressed my inside. He moved outward, stroking the sensual nub with his thumb, then covered my entire crotch with his palm, massaging and then penetrating again with his fingers, going deeper and deeper. I arched up, allowing more access to his movements, and gasped with growing desire. My moans came one after another as the pace quickened. I clutched the sheet with my hands, my lungs running out of air.

"Don't hold back. Scream, come, let me feel it," Alex commanded as he continued to drive me crazy.

"Aaah... Alex..."

My whole body trembled, and pleasure spread spasms through my lower abdomen. But before I could come to my senses, Frai entered me quickly and deeply with one thrust. His hot shaft rubbed against the walls inside my still shortening orgasmic vagina.

His chest pressed against my back, and his hand gripped my thigh. I pressed my ass against him to meet his thrusts.

The thrusts became more rhythmic and harder. Alex's breathing merged with his moans. He moved his hand from my hip to my waist, digging into my skin and thrusting into me. His lips caressed my neck, and his tongue left a wet trail on my skin. We were both already at the peak of pleasure.

When he froze, letting out a long, hoarse moan, his

whole body tensing and shuddering, I began to move slowly, stretching out his pleasure.

"This is how every morning should be," my man said breathlessly, kissing my shoulder gently.

"I guess I'm okay with that," I said with a smile, pressing myself against his hot, sweaty body.

I wanted to melt into his arms and not let go, to stay with him forever, but soon enough, Benjamin knocked on our door, reminding Alex that it was time for them to leave.

Kissing me on the shoulder, Frai quickly packed up and left to run errands. I remembered that I had plans for the day, too. So I got ready and went out into the hallway.

The house was as noisy as a beehive. Everyone was running around errands for Bennett. Tonight, Lika had planned a dinner party at Alex's mansion in honor of my recovery. Since my parents would be flying home tomorrow, she decided to take the opportunity to get everyone together.

In the hallway, Sarah, the maid, ran into me. She was holding a vase. Colliding with me she couldn't keep it, and the vase fell, smashing to the floor. Bennett appeared behind her like a genie out of a lamp. His glare made even my hair stand on end.

Before the manager could say anything, I attempted to save the girl.

"Oh, I'm so sorry, Sarah. I didn't notice you. Are you all right?" and turning to Bennett, added, "I hope it wasn't Alex's favourite vase that was broken through my fault?"

"I don't think it was your fault, Miss Anna. Somebody ought to be more careful," said Bennett, with a meaningful look at the maid.

"The important thing is that everyone's safe. Don't worry about the vase. I'll personally report to Mr. Frai about the loss. As you already have too much to worry about," I parried, winking at Sarah.

The girl thanked me silently and started picking up the

shards. At the same moment, Grace's screams came from the kitchen. Apparently, someone had mixed up the order and brought something wrong. All the manager's attention turned in that direction, and he left us with a quick step.

Today, I had to supervise the correct arrangement of tables, their serving, and the decoration of the hall, which I did with particular pleasure.

Everyone was very excited about the upcoming event, as the house owner was not a big fan of noisy companies. The maximum that could be held in the mansion was a business dinner with important clients, and rarely. I even wondered how Lika had managed to persuade her brother to do it. After the attack, Alex was literally obsessed with security and was very worried about me, strengthening security to the point of insanity. He even asked me if I would agree to get a tracking chip under my skin, and of course, after that, he got a one-way ticket for an extended stroll afterward.

Chapter 33

Julie arrived just in time. I had already finished my chores, and all I had to do was get ready for the party. We settled into my bedroom, laid out our outfits, checked that everything fit together, and started on our makeup.

"How are things with Alex?" My friend asked.

"Everything is pretty good. Although Alex keeps disappearing, he's trying hard to make time for us."

"Have you already talked to him?" Julie asked seriously.

"No. Yesterday, I brought up another topic that's been bothering me."

"What was the topic?" My friend asked in surprise.

"Pretty personal," I said, blushing, not wanting to go into details.

Even though Julie and I had talked about many things,

I wanted to keep some of them just between Alex and me.

"I see," Julie smiled and continued to work her magic on me.

"It was crazy easy for me to talk to Alex about anything. But I don't have the courage to ask about the bet. We're no longer on schedule. Maybe it means the end of the game or a tie," I suggested.

"Maybe we should talk to Lika. She should be in the loop," Julie offered.

"Not a good idea. I should be talking to him, not acting behind his back."

"That's a good idea, but don't take too long. It's definitely torturing you," Jules said and pressed her lips together.

"And how are things with you and Benny?" I decided to change the subject.

"He and I have an age difference, but I don't feel it when we talk. I feel like I'm behind a rock wall with him. I don't know, but I think I'm in love."

"It's so wonderful. I'm so happy for you."

"Well, both of us, we're finally going to have a happy ending."

I got up and gave my friend a big hug. I wish things had worked out for the best for both of us.

My makeup was ready. With curiosity, I peered into the mirror and gasped. It was like a girl I didn't know was standing before me. My eyes were glowing, shimmering from green to blue. My hair was gathered in a neat bundle with released, twisted strands. Julie gave me a chic smokey eye, emphasizing the expressiveness of my eyes, highlighted my eyebrows, and applied a pale pink lipstick to my lips so as not to overdo the bright accents.

I wore a lacy red dress delivered to me by courier at lunchtime. It was a gift from Alex. The dress was floor-length, made of a thin and almost weightless fabric. A chiffon train from the waist added a lushness to the look. And there were red high-heeled shoes on the feet, which perfectly complemented the elegant image of the lady in red.

"You look gorgeous. You could be on the cover of a magazine."

My friend took my hand and started spinning me around. The mood was marvelous. I couldn't believe it was my reality. It seemed like nothing in the whole world could mar this day.

Julie looked cool, too. She was wearing an emerald dress. Combined with her fiery red hair in neat waves, it looked stunning.

"Benjamin's jaw will drop when he sees you," I concluded.

"I can't wait to meet him. I hope to impress him."

"I'm sure you will."

"When I hear gentle words and compliments from a man as rugged as Beni, I just swoon," she said dreamily.

Her phone vibrated. She read the message and blushed thickly. I'd never seen her so embarrassed before. Julie was pretty hard to get her to blush.

"Anna, I need to run. I'll wait for you downstairs. My man's already here, and he's eager to meet me."

"Go ahead. I'll be down in five minutes," I said with a laugh as my friend ran off to meet her lover.

I still had to put on my earrings to finish packing. They were the cherry on the cake. The massive ruby earrings were a gift from my beloved grandmother that I'd gotten for my eighteenth birthday.

I sat at the table, my back to the door, looking in a small mirror and trying to fasten the clasp on my jewelry. Suddenly, I heard someone come in behind.

"Did you forget something?" I asked without turning around, mistaking the visitor for Julie.

"Yes, I forgot something very important. And I hope to get it back today."

When I heard that voice, I felt like I'd been electrocuted. I turned around and couldn't believe my eyes.

"How are you here? And most importantly, why?" I asked in complete shock.

"I'm here to tell you the truth and open your eyes."

"What truth? What are you talking about?"

"Alex's true feelings for you. I want to dispel your naiveté at his sudden change and show you his real face."

"Dan, you ran away months ago and never contacted me. And now, you show up out of nowhere and want me to listen to you?" I said harshly.

"I was wrong to leave. It really was my mistake. But then I wasn't given a choice, your lover sent me far away so he wouldn't have competition."

"Dan, look, the last few months have been very difficult. And I don't have the energy for your revelations right now," I said irritably.

"Anna, have you ever wondered why your life became so complicated overnight?" continued the uninvited guest.

"Let me guess. Is it Alex's fault? Is that what you mean? But as it turns out, our meeting is more of Lika's merit," I said and stood up.

"What about your involvement in this bet? If memory serves me correctly, you were against it and didn't want to be a part of it."

"It was just a matter of circumstance. Alex didn't force me into anything. It was my choice and my decision," I said confidently and came closer to Dan.

I wanted to show him that I'm not the same fragile girl that I was.

"Hmm... Circumstances, you say. And it didn't bother you how all the events happened, one after another, forcing you to come to the only savior? You were never stupid. You're telling me you didn't even consider the idea that everything happened not by accident but by design?"

Breathless, I didn't believe Dan's words, but there was an uneasy feeling inside.

"How did he pull this off so fast?" I asked, not so eagerly.

"It's Mr. Frai himself. He can do anything. He has a detailed file on everyone. For example, your dossier was collected by the end of your first day of acquaintance," Dan said with emotion and anger. "Your ex-husband didn't think of taking your money on his own. A friend tipped him off. Guess whose tip? And isn't it strange how a buyer showed up for the café when it wasn't even for sale? Well, the salon you worked at didn't close down by accident. And everything you did failed at Alex's behest. So tell me, was that really your choice? Or was it desperation that drove you to desperate action?"

My legs felt heavy, and I sat on the edge of the bed to keep from falling. The same thought kept popping into my head before. It was too suspicious, but I pushed it away with all my might.

Could Alex really have done that? Ran through my head.

"It's a lie, and I refuse to believe it. I don't know why you're doing this, but please leave me alone," I said and shook my head from side to side.

Dan silently pulled out his phone and turned on the recording.

"What the fuck? Why did you do that?"

"Maybe the problem is that I'm more human! And you starting to look more and more like a robot?"

"Who asked you to get involved? Everything was carefully planned. She'd have come to me on her own, and it would be a win-win. I'd solve her problems with being here and give her money. She wouldn't need anything. And what do you want with this unremarkable person? What's so special about her?"

"Do you hear what you're saying? First, she's a living person. You didn't see her that night. Anna was broken and lost, frozen through...Lika is right. You created this company, successful and profitable. You put so much work into it. But you also put your whole soul here without a trace. You've lost yourself, man, and I'm sorry you don't realize that."

"I don't remember you thinking the same thing when you asked me to be one of your club's investors."

"I've paid you back in full. I'm out of debt. And know what? I'm not going to give Anna to you. That girl is sweet, bright, and kind. Whatever you're up to, she'll be under my protection."

"I think I see what this is all about now. You've fallen in love."

"Even if I did, it's none of your business."

"You know I won't back down, and I'll do anything. There's something more important at stake than a stupid crush."

"I may not have the power and opportunities you have, but I'm more like a human being than an emotionless machine."

I listened and still couldn't believe it. Alex's angry voice on that tape and his words had me in a complete stupor.

"Why would you do that?" I asked, almost in a whisper as I recovered from the shock.

"To let you know the truth, and I'm afraid that's not all."

With every word that Dan said, everything inside me turned upside down. It turned out that Alex had sent his friend to some island, leaving him there without papers, though in perfect living condition. With his charm, the blond Casanova had bewitched a local girl from the administration of the hotel where he was staying, and with her help, he was able to get out, not without difficulty.

Everything about this story was shocking, but most of all, Alex's coolness was astounding. There was a clear calculation in his actions.

Dan also knew the answer about the bet which has been plaguing me so much. I wondered what Frai and Lika had decided. The blond guy had an acquaintance who worked for Angelica, and she'd told him that Alex and his sister, due to unforeseen circumstances, had put everything on hold until I was fully recovered. And then everything was supposed to back to the old scenario.

"You see, he will never give up that piece of land. And when the villa goes to his possession, Alex will forget everything and fly there on the very next flight, conveniently forgetting about his supposed feelings."

"But why is it so important to him?" I felt tears welling

up in my throat.

"He didn't even tell you about it, but he swears his love," Dan was quiet for a second, but then asked, "Say, do you know what fate befell your ex-husband thanks to the same person?"

A chill ran down my spine at the mention of my ex-husband.

"No. I don't know," I answered tiredly, crushed by all this information.

"Alex, when he found out that you'd filed for divorce, made a couple of phone calls and organized an unforgettable life of adventure for Max. Your ex-husband first lost his job and later his residency permit and was deported. Can you imagine how hard that must have been on his parents?"

"It's all too much," I felt dizzy, and something in my chest started to press.

"Anna, my car is outside the gate. Come with me. I've prepared everything. We'll escape, and he won't get us. That man doesn't deserve your love. He'll just trample it," Dan continued to push his line, ignoring my condition.

"No, I don't want to run away. I needed at least to look in his eyes and hear his explanation."

Even after finding out everything, I couldn't fall out of love with Alex overnight. It was killing me inside, but I decided at least to give him a chance to explain.

"He's going to mess with your head again," Dan walked over, kneeling in front of me and taking my hands in his, "Anna, all this time I've been thinking about you. Give me a chance. Unlike him, I have real feelings. I love you."

"You didn't tell me everything to open my eyes," I pulled my hands away and got up from the bed. "You just want to take me away from him. That's not love. A second ago, I was so happy. And now there's just a giant hole in my heart."

Dan was so diligent in slinging mud at Alex that I was

disgusted to be in the same room with him.

With a quick step, I left the room and headed for the stairs. As I walked down the stairs, I felt my legs shaking and nausea coming on.

I was disgusted with myself that after everything I had heard, I didn't run away but went with little hope that everything could still be fixed. Tears came to my eyes, but I tried my best to hold them back.

I immediately found Alex in the crowd, in a black tuxedo, with a glass of whiskey in his hands. He was standing next to his sister, with whom they were chatting animatedly. Lika noticed me and elbowed her brother, pointing in my direction. His eyes shone, and setting down his glass, he hurried in my direction.

"I was already getting worried. Everyone's been here a long time. But the hostess is still missing," Frai gave me his hand. "You're so beautiful."

"Thank you," I said with difficulty.

"Are you all right?"

There was a look of concern, even fear, on the face of the man I loved. He stared at my face, waiting for an answer, but I had nothing to say. I stared into his eyes, trying to figure out if he was playing or if he really was able to love.

Our silent pause was interrupted by Lika.

"What a gorgeous couple you are. I can admire forever, but I have a toast."

Angelica rose on the first step so that she could be better seen. Standing between us, she began to speak louder so that everyone could hear her.

"For the last few years, I've been living in the hope that Alex would have someone in his life who could wake him up and make him live life to the fullest. And thankfully, I was able to live to see those days. I want to raise a glass to our dear Anna. Thank you for being you."

Everyone applauded and raised their glasses. Alex continued to stare at me. His closeness was hard for me, and tears kept choking me.

It was useless to lie to myself. I loved him with all my being. And he loved me too but in his own way. Even after everything Dan had told me, he was my air. I literally breathed him. But to stay, knowing that I would never mean as much to him as he meant to me, knowing that I would always come second to his job, villa, and other important things, would be even more painful.

Taking my hand from Alex, I headed for the exit. I wanted to run away, no matter where, certainly not with Dan, but at least just away from this house for starters.

Chapter 34

Halfway to the exit, Lika stopped me by grabbing my arm.

"Anna, what are you doing? You're not wearing your face? What's wrong?"

"I just need some fresh air. I'm fine, don't worry," I blatantly lied.

Dodging Lika, I walked to the front door. But I heard a voice behind me.

"Before you run away from me, I'd really like to give you a little gift."

Alex spoke loudly from where he stood. His gaze was downcast. Bennett walked over to me and held out a black folder.

"These are the documents for the Villa Delrado. The thing I thought I wanted more than anything in life. But after being one step away from losing you, I realized that you are my life. Now you're the owner and can do whatever you want with these documents," Alex said.

I looked at Lika in complete bewilderment. She nodded her head in confirmation of Alex's words.

I opened the folder. It really contained the documents

for the villa, registered in my name. While I was looking at the documents, Alex came close to me.

"This morning, I went to see Lika and accepted defeat. I don't care about the consequences or anything in the world except you," Alex spoke calmly, but he was scared. I could feel it. "Can we go outside and talk?"

I nodded in agreement, and we walked outside. We sat down on the steps in front of the house, and I decided to start the dialog first:

"If you accepted defeat, where did you get the documents from?"

"A gift from Lika. She said she'd achieved exactly what she'd dreamed of. And that was her only objective in this bet."

"What will happen to the company? Will you lose controlling interest?" I was asking questions while my heart was trying to jump out of my chest.

"When I announced to Lika about accepting the loss, I was mentally prepared for it. But she refused all the conditions and handed over the documents, knowing they no longer had the same value to me as before, the same as my company. I meant what I said. You mean more to me than anything in this world," Alex spoke still calmly, but I could see the anxiety in his eyes.

"But why was this villa so important to you?"

"It's because of my father. I wanted to take revenge on him and burn the villa to the ground and make him suffer. It's a particular piece of land for him."

"Did he own the villa?"

"It used to be. But for Angelica's coming of age, he gave it to her. He was sure I wouldn't reach the land that way."

"But what's so special about these vineyards?"

"His thriving business began with this plot of land. And for it, my father left the family for a mistress who helped him buy the title. And before he left, he sold the house, leaving me and my mom practically on the street because he didn't have enough collateral. He offered to let me go with him, but I would never leave my mom alone."

"It's awful. How can someone do that to their child?" It was more of a rhetorical question.

"The real horror awaited ahead."

"Your scars?"

"Yes."

Alex shrank even more. He was having a hard time saying the words.

"You don't have to say anything if you're not ready," I said and looked into his eyes.

"I want to, but I need your support."

He took my hand and pulled me to him. I sat on his lap and rested my head against his chest, hugging him tightly.

"When we were left without a home, our only option was to move to my grandmother's small old house. There, a neighbor began courting Mom. She avoided him, but Grandma insisted on their relationship because "it's not good for a woman to be alone with a child," that's literally. After the wedding, the new husband first outlived my grandmother. Then the nightmare began. He started drinking a lot, and worst of all, he started raising his hand to my mom. I always tried to protect my mom, but unfortunately, it wasn't easy."

I felt Alex's heart racing. As he told his story, he was reliving it all over again.

"One day, when I came home, I saw my mom in tears with a busted lip. Standing over her was her husband, who had been totally drunk. I was so angry. I jumped on him. I wanted to kill him, but at that moment, he was physically superior to me and could easily throw me away like a puppy. I fell and couldn't get up right away."

Alex was holding back tears. There was so much pain in him, and he didn't let it out. He kept it deep inside him, punishing himself as if what had happened was his fault.

"My attack made him furious. He grabbed a belt with a metal buckle and started hitting me on the back. With a scream, mom rushed to me in an attempt to protect. The scumbag, regaining his senses, rushed away. When my mom saw the consequences of his blows, her heart could not stand it," every word Alex gave with difficulty. "I blacked out almost immediately from the intense pain."

Alex continued to hold back tears, and I pressed myself into him. I desperately wanted to take away some of his pain.

"Grace found us and called an ambulance. When I came to, I found out my mom was gone," Alex finished, holding back the last of his strength.

"Let go. Please don't hold back the tears. Let the pain come out. Live it and share it with me. You've carried it all alone for too long already," I said carefully.

I took his face in my hands and pressed myself against him, feeling the hot tears roll down his cheeks in unison with mine.

We sat like that for a long time until he broke the silence with a question:

"I've completely opened up to you. And so I'm asking you to answer honestly. Did you want to run away with Dan?"

"Did you know he was here?" I was genuinely surprised.

"The whole house is under surveillance. There are guards on every corner. He couldn't have gotten in here without my permission."

"But why did you let him? Didn't you take care of his disappearance?"

"Everything he told you is true. I wanted to tell you myself. You have no idea how many times I tried to work up the courage to do it. But every time, fear overcame me. I've known about Dan's return for about a week now. So I decided to give him the right to tell you. I know it doesn't sound very fair, but I wouldn't have done it any other way," he paused and added, "You still haven't answered my question."

"Yes, I wanted to run away, but definitely not with him. There can't be another man in my life but you," I said and pressed myself against Alex.

"You have no idea how glad I am to hear that," Frai said with relief.

"Al, Dan also said that you interfered with Max's fate and got him deported. Is that true, too?"

"Yes, and he was lucky I'd limited myself to that. When I found out he'd raised his hand on you," Alex tensed, paused, and continued, "I regretted that I'd limited myself only to that."

"But how did you find out?" My eyes widened in surprise.

"Julie told me when we were in the hospital."

"What a friend," I mumbled.

"She's a good friend, though sometimes she doesn't give the best advice," Alex said and pressed his lips together.

"Are you talking about how she suggested I check what you really cared about?" I asked with a smile.

"Mm-hmm. And by the way, I'm really glad you didn't listen to her. However, later on, you found an adventure on your head anyway."

"Well, it's more of a mutual fault."

"Not really. But I'm in no mood to argue. I'm happy you're okay. And now I have the opportunity to hold you tightly in my arms."

Covering his lips in a kiss, I wanted to burst into pieces at the realization that Dan was wrong. Alex was able to change. He loved me as much as I loved him.

He's mine, and I'm his, and that's the way it will be as long as my heart beats. My mind raced through my head.

I wish I could say that all the hardships were over and a happy and peaceful life was ahead of us, but in fact, at this point, our story was just beginning.

www.ingramcontent.com/pod-product-compliance
Lightning Source LLC
LaVergne TN
LVHW020054210726
843507LV00016B/2265